"You shoul

Those m

can stay

The words came out on their own. Even as he said them, it seemed as if someone else was doing so. Sara looked just as surprised to hear them.

"Just for tonight. Until you figure out something else." Part of him wondered who he was saying it for, her or himself.

"Okay, thank you. Let me get a few things." Jake knew letting her stay with him was the right thing to do. She shouldn't be alone, not in her condition. That didn't stop him from wanting to call her back and revoke the offer. The uneasiness had returned with a vengeance, clawing at his insides with greater ferocity, for entirely different reasons than before.

Because he'd seen something else, too, shimmering faintly in her big brown eyes.

Gratitude.

And he knew more than ever that he'd finally made a mistake he'd been avoiding from the first time he'd seen the pregnant woman next door.

He'd invited her into his life. And now there was no turning back.

KERRY CONNOR

A STRANGER'S BABY

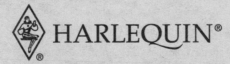

TORONTO • NEW YORK • LONDON
AMSTERDAM • PARIS • SYDNEY • HAMBURG
STOCKHOLM • ATHENS • TOKYO • MILAN • MADRID
PRAGUE • WARSAW • BUDAPEST • AUCKLAND

This book was particularly challenging to write,
and is dedicated with my deepest thanks to the editors
without whom it wouldn't exist: Sean Mackiewicz,
for making my dream of writing for Intrigue a reality and
for guiding me through the process with my first
two books; Denise Zaza, for the opportunity and
for believing in my work; and Allison Lyons, for
her kindness and patience, and for the words of
encouragement when I needed them the most. Thank you.

ISBN-13: 978-0-373-88903-7
ISBN-10:   0-373-88903-8

Recycling programs
for this product may
not exist in your area.

A STRANGER'S BABY

www.eHarlequin.com

Printed in U.S.A.

ABOUT THE AUTHOR

A lifelong mystery reader, Kerry Connor first discovered romantic suspense by reading Harlequin Intrigue books and is thrilled to be writing for the line. Kerry lives and writes in Southern California.

Books by Kerry Connor

HARLEQUIN INTRIGUE
1067—STRANGERS IN THE NIGHT
1094—BEAUTIFUL STRANGER
1129—A STRANGER'S BABY

CAST OF CHARACTERS

Sara Carson—One reckless night left her pregnant with a stranger's baby.

Jake Armstrong—A man who believes he knows nothing about family is the only one who can help the pregnant woman next door.

Mark—The mystery man who fathered Sara's child.

Roger Halloran—He was searching for answers and more than willing to use Sara to get them.

Kendra Rogan—She said that helping young people was her top priority, but did her noble claims mask darker intentions?

Noah Brooks—The friendly young man proved a ready source of information, but did he know more than he revealed?

Adam Quinn—A man who knew when it was time to move on, but whose true motives remained in question.

Chapter One

Someone was in the house.

Sara stared into the bedroom's darkness, wide awake when she'd been asleep seconds earlier. She wasn't sure what had woken her from the first good sleep she'd had in weeks, any more than she knew why she was suddenly certain she was no longer alone in her home.

She simply knew.

One hand instantly moved to her belly. The other reached into the bedside table. Her fingers closed around the gun she'd put there for this very reason. Protection. A single woman living alone needed some way to defend herself.

Careful not to make a sound, Sara pulled the weapon to her and strained to hear any signs of an intruder. The pounding of her heart in her ears drowned out everything else.

Even so, she didn't think she detected anything. There was only the steady drone of the air conditioner, cranked up high because she was always hot these days. Eyes wide, she tried to spot what didn't belong there in the darkness. Nothing moved, nothing seemed out of place.

Still, the certainty remained.

She slowly uncurled herself from the body pillow that was the only thing that had let her get any sleep the past several months and rolled onto her back. The lamp switch was just out of arm's reach. She'd have to push herself up to get to it. Or should she even turn it on? Would the light scare off whoever might be out there or simply alert them to her presence and wakefulness, especially if she made too much noise shifting on the bed?

She should have gotten a dog, a big, scary one trained to ward off intruders. A dog would know if someone was in the house, confirming or dismissing her fears instead of leaving her searching for something that might not even be there. But she hadn't known what she'd do with the dog when she went to the hospital. There was no one she could ask, and if she went into labor suddenly, the dog would be left behind alone in the house for days—

Her frenzied thoughts must have distracted her from her silent vigil. One moment the doorway yawned with emptiness. The next, so suddenly it seemed to have appeared in the time it took her to blink, a dark figure stood there.

He made no sound as he moved into the room, seeming to float through the passageway. Two others followed close behind.

She took no joy in the knowledge she wasn't imagining things. Terror gripped her so suddenly she couldn't restrain a gasp.

The sharply indrawn breath didn't go unnoticed. The figures came to an abrupt stop, hovering there in the darkness.

"You're awake," she heard a low voice murmur in surprise.

"That's right," she said calmly, somehow managing to keep the fear out of her voice when every instinct wanted to scream. "And you're trespassing."

They began to drift closer again, undeterred by her words or her awareness. Suddenly she realized the one in the lead was raising his hand. The pale threads of moonlight peeking through the slats of her window blinds glinted off something he was holding.

Her heart jumped as recognition slammed into her.

A needle.

She instinctively spread her fingers wider on her abdomen, as though the small gesture could provide greater cover, more protection, to the child inside her.

"Don't worry, Sara." The voice came again, closer now, softened in a parody of a soothing tone. "This won't hurt at all."

Her response was to cock the weapon in her hand, the sound loud in the silence.

The figures froze.

She aimed right at the head of the one with the needle. "This will."

And fired.

JAKE ARMSTRONG EASED HIMSELF out of the truck, first his good left leg, then the right that seemed to have failed him yet again. He tried to keep the weight off his right foot, gingerly setting it on the pavement and leaning on the left.

It didn't help. A sharp pain shot down the limb starting at the knee. Gripping the door, he sucked in a breath through gritted teeth. He'd taken two pills as soon as he'd exited the all-night drugstore, downing them without water, needing them too much, hating that he did. For all the good they'd done him. The pills must not have kicked in yet.

Or maybe he'd waited too long and now would have to wait that much longer for them to start working. He hadn't bothered refilling the prescription after he'd run out weeks ago, thinking he didn't need the medicine anymore.

So much for that.

Damn. He'd thought he was doing well, too, enough so that he'd felt confident ignoring the initial twinges that had probably indicated something was wrong. He was used to fighting through pain. He was running farther and harder every day. He felt stronger. His old doctors would say he was pushing himself too hard, and for no reason. That he was lucky to be walking at all after they'd put his knee back together.

"Damn doctors," he grumbled under his breath. "Don't know what they're talking about." Which was exactly why they were no longer his doctors.

At least there was nobody else out on the street at two o'clock in the morning to see him hobbling around. Not for the first time, he was glad he'd gotten a place in this town outside of Boston, rather than staying in the city. The neighborhood remained still and quiet, every house darkened for the night.

He was about to slam the door shut when an explosion cut through the air, catching him off guard, causing him to stumble. Leaning into the door, he whipped his head toward the noise. He knew the sound of gunfire. It came in rapid succession, one shot after another after another.

He didn't have to look far to determine the origin. The shots were coming from inside the house next door.

The house where the pregnant woman lived.

The bottle of pills fell from his hand, forgotten, as he reached for his cell and stabbed in the numbers. The sounds of the gunshots continued to hang in the air, uninterrupted by fresh ones.

"9-1-1. What's your emergency?"

"There's gunfire coming from my neighbor's house. She's a pregnant woman. Lives alone."

"What's the address?" the dispatcher asked with admirable calm.

He quickly gave it to her, answering her follow-up questions on autopilot as he surveyed the house. No lights were on in the building; there was no way to see inside. No further sounds came from within. The closest streetlamp was on the other side of the road, its steady beam barely reaching the lawn. The driveway was empty, her vehicle likely parked inside the garage. The house itself remained shrouded in shadows. He stared into them, but detected no signs of movement.

The echo of the gunfire faded from his ears, leaving nothing but a silence so absolute that he wondered, for a heartbeat, if he'd imagined what he'd thought he'd heard. He dismissed the thought a second later. He knew what he'd heard. It had been gunfire.

Which only made the endless silence that followed and lack of movement inside the house more disturbing.

As if from a great distance, he heard the dispatcher assuring him the police were on their way and asking him to stay on the line. The final words barely reached him. He was already hanging up, moving forward as fast as his gimpy leg would let him.

It would take the police a while to get there, and even longer for an ambulance if one wasn't called until after they arrived and determined it was necessary. She could be hurt. She could be dying, her and the baby. He couldn't just stand there. He had to do something.

He stalked around the edge of the lawn, not wanting to cross directly and get too close too soon. Every second he braced himself, ready for another shot to come from the house, prepared to duck.

It never came. Reaching the front path, he followed it to the door. Hoping he wasn't making a mistake, he pounded on it with his fist.

"Hey—" he started to call out, only to stop abruptly, suddenly realizing he didn't know her name. She hadn't introduced herself after he'd moved in last month, apparently no more interested in getting to know him than he was her. They'd exchanged nothing more than brief glances across their lawns whenever they both happened to be in front of their respective homes. She'd give him a polite nod, a short, shy smile as her gaze skittered away. She was pretty, from what he could tell, but evidently not social. Not that he could judge. He wasn't, either.

"Everything okay in there?" he asked instead.

He waited for a light to flicker on inside or for her to answer the door.

A full minute passed. Nothing happened.

He repeated the knock and the call, to no effect.

The lack of a response only stoked his tension. He tried the knob and wasn't surprised to find it locked.

Something was going on. He had to find another way inside the house.

From what he remembered, there was another door in the back of the building. He gave a quick check in the front window. Seeing nothing, he made his way around the side of the house. The other windows were no more illuminating, in more ways than one.

He knocked on the back door, then tried the knob. It turned in his hand. The door swung open silently at his touch. He stayed by the wall, out of view of anyone inside, waiting to see what happened.

Nothing did. Silence resounded.

"Hello?" he called into the darkness.

No response.

He slowly moved through the doorway, watching for any sign of trouble. Spotting none, he reached over and flipped the light switch, revealing his neighbor's kitchen. It was empty.

"Hello?" he called again.

Still no response. He ventured farther, keeping his eyes moving in every direction, senses on high alert. The kitchen opened onto a darkened hallway, the gloom pierced by a faint light glowing from one of the rooms. A quick glance in either direction told him the hallway was empty. Reassured, he turned and headed toward the light.

"Lady, are you okay?"

Even as he said it, the floor creaked beneath his foot, betraying his location.

"Stay back!" a voice ordered, drawing him to a halt. "I still have a couple bullets left and I'm more than ready to use them. I'm calling 9-1-1."

The voice was strong, firm and undeniably female. He half wondered if he should ask who he was talking to, because there was no way that hardened tone could be coming from the mouth of the woman with the shy smile and retreating gaze. But who else would be calling 9-1-1? Did she have someone staying with her? He hadn't noticed anyone, but then, he hadn't been paying attention.

"I already did. The cops are on their way."

She didn't say anything to that. He stood stock-still, listening to the ragged sounds of her breathing inside the room.

"Look, I'm just going to poke my head around the corner so you can see me. I'd appreciate it if you didn't blow it off."

Another long silence, then a reluctant "Okay."

Her tone wasn't reassuring. He wondered for a few seconds if he really wanted to risk it. It seemed like he'd gone past the point of no return now. Taking a breath, he leaned over with painstaking slowness and pushed his head into the doorway.

As promised and suspected, he found himself staring down the barrel of a gun. Even as he entered the doorway, his eyes focused on her, she made a nearly imperceptible correction, keeping them right in her sights. He had the feeling she had every intention of putting a bullet straight between them if he looked at her funny.

He did his best to ignore the gun, no easy feat, and met the steady gaze behind it. This was his neighbor, all right. His first impression was that he'd been right. She was pretty, even more than he'd expected. She had soft features, her face full and round, probably more than usual due to her condition. Not a classic beauty, but definitely attractive.

There was nothing soft about her expression. Dark brown eyes met his, unblinking.

The hands that held the gun were steady, as unwavering as her stare. She might be on edge, but there was no doubt she knew exactly what she was doing, and was ready to do whatever else she thought she had to.

"Hi," he said lamely. "We haven't officially been introduced. I'm Jake Armstrong.

I moved into the house next door last month. I just came over to make sure you're okay."

Her gaze raked over his face, as though scrutinizing every inch for any sign he wasn't who he said he was or who he appeared to be. He waited, hoping to high hell he passed her inspection.

Finally, just when he was about to coax her to do just that, she lowered the gun. Not entirely. No more than a few inches really. Her finger didn't release the trigger, leaving the impression she was prepared to jerk the weapon back up and fire at the slightest provocation.

Still, it was a start.

Her expression didn't relax, either. Her gaze narrowed, slowly traveling down the length of him and back again. She gave a small nod, as though satisfied. "You're not one of them."

"Who?"

"The people who broke in to my house. You're too big."

Not the first time he'd heard that one. "Who was it? What did they want?"

"I don't know."

A troubled note entered her voice, and the hard lines of her expression softened slightly, betraying the first hint of the fear she must have been feeling. She eased her left hand off her weapon and moved it onto the swell of her belly, as though reassuring herself it was still there, still safe.

His eyes tracked the gesture, a feeling of dread pooling in the pit of his stomach. The obvious answer would have been robbery. That she hadn't said so must mean she believed it was something else. Something related to her baby, judging from the way her hand clutched her stomach.

Why would someone break in to her house because of her baby?

A few answers came to mind, none of them good.

And he had to wonder just what would have happened here if she hadn't had that gun.

Chapter Two

"I'm telling you, I was not dreaming."

Sara did her best to fight her rising impatience, but was still unable to keep the aggravation completely out of her tone.

The police officer who'd finally responded to her neighbor's 9-1-1 call gave her that condescending look that was the cause of most of her irritation. Then he opened his mouth and delivered the source of the rest of it.

"I'm sorry, Ms. Carson, but like I said, we checked the whole house and weren't able to find any signs that anyone else was here. There's no indication the door was tampered with, no footprints inside or outside the house. No blood or any other reason to believe you shot anybody."

"They ducked and ran," she said for what seemed like the millionth time.

The officer—Dawson, she recalled him introducing himself—didn't even acknowledge the interruption. "None of your neighbors saw anything, and you say nothing was taken."

"That's because I scared them off before they had the chance," she returned. "Not that I think they were here to steal anything."

"Right," he said on a sigh. "The needle. Are you sure that's what you saw? If the lights were off, in the dark…"

"It was shiny, and they said 'This won't hurt.' It was a needle."

"Do you know of any reason why someone might break in and try to harm you or your baby?"

"No."

"Who else has a key?"

"No one."

"And you're sure you locked the back door before you went to bed?"

"Yes."

The officer sighed again. "Ms. Carson, you said you haven't been sleeping well. A woman living alone, in your condition, it's understandable you might have a bad dream, or think you see something that isn't there—"

"I'm pregnant, not deranged."

His eyebrows went up and his gaze slid

away, an expression that clearly said "Is there a difference?" She hadn't missed the wedding ring on his finger and wondered briefly if he had kids. If so, she hoped he'd been more empathetic to his wife than he was being with her. Or maybe that experience was the cause of his current attitude.

Sara shot a glance at the other officer standing in the living-room doorway. He had a small smirk on his face, with slightly more impatience. She wouldn't be getting any help from him.

She returned her attention to Dawson. "I know what happened," she said stubbornly.

"I know you believe that. We just have to go by the evidence."

"So you're not going to do anything?"

Dawson held out his hands in a helpless gesture. "I'm not sure what I can do. Even if there was somebody here, we don't have any way of tracking them down unless there's something else you're not telling me."

Even if there was, what was the point? It wasn't as if what she had told him had done her any good. "There's not."

"Look at it this way. If somebody did break in, they probably won't be coming back. I'd say you did a darn good job scaring them off. They won't want to mess with you again."

"I guess," she muttered, unconvinced for reasons she couldn't quite explain, but which scared her all the same.

"Tell you what. I'll have somebody drive by a couple times the rest of the night, just to make sure everything looks okay."

There was a definite note of finality in his tone. Even as he said it, he was rising from his seat. Clearly they'd wasted enough time on the delusional pregnant woman.

"Fine," she said begrudgingly. She didn't bother to rise with him. They'd be able to make it to the next county by the time she hoisted herself from the chair.

Touching the brim of his hat, he offered one last "Ma'am" and headed to the door, following the other officer out.

As soon as they were gone, Sara wiped a hand over her face and released the frustrated breath she'd been holding. She knew she hadn't imagined what had happened. Someone had broken in to her home, someone who'd intended to harm her. There just didn't seem to be any way to prove it.

Which meant she was on her own to figure out what to do now. Not that that was anything new.

A soft tap against the door frame startled her. Her eyes flew to the entryway, her heart in her throat. Her neighbor stood there, the sight instantly reassuring. Jake, he'd said his name was. Just like the first time she'd seen him, she was struck by his sheer size, which was only emphasized in the smaller confines of her house. The man was massive, well over six feet tall and brawny, his shoulders filling the frame, his head barely clearing the ceiling. His size was such a defining characteristic that she'd had no trouble knowing he wasn't involved in the break-in. She would have recognized this mountain coming at her in the dark.

From the few glimpses she'd had of him when they'd nodded to each other in passing, he'd struck her as deeply intimidating. Up close, he was slightly less so, if only because she could see his face more clearly. He wasn't exactly handsome, but there was definitely something appealing in the blunt masculinity of his features. He'd always had this fierce expression on his face. She'd never seen him smile. He wasn't now, either.

"I guess I'll take off, too," he said. "I just wanted to make sure you're okay."

"I'm fine," she said, because it was easier than trying to convince someone else otherwise. *Just hallucinating, evidently.* "I never thanked you for calling 9-1-1 and coming over to check things out."

He nodded shortly, lowering his eyes, as though embarrassed by her gratitude. "Don't mention it. What are neighbors for, right?"

"Right," she echoed with a pang of guilt, all too aware she hadn't really lived up to that unspoken rule. She'd done what she always did, kept to herself. Because it was easier. Because she was a coward. But then, until tonight, so had he.

"The back door is locked. I can get the front on my way out."

His way out. He was leaving. And she'd be alone. "Great," she said, her tension tangling in knots in her stomach.

Her nervousness must have come across loud and clear. "If you don't feel safe, maybe you shouldn't stay here. Call a friend."

Sara shook her head, embarrassed to admit the truth. "I don't know anyone around here."

If he wondered why she didn't when she'd lived here longer than he had, he didn't comment on it. His expression didn't change. "Get a hotel room for the night."

"Maybe I will," she said halfheartedly, already thinking of all the things she'd have to do. It would take her a while to get some things together—another reason she should have put her overnight bag for the hospital together by now—and she'd have to call a cab to take her, since she didn't trust herself to drive in her current state. Given how fast she moved these days, it would probably be dawn by the time she made it to a hotel. Hardly worth the trouble, since she didn't think they would try anything in broad daylight.

It was the hours until then that worried her.

"Well, if you stay, I wouldn't worry about it," her neighbor said. "You'll be fine."

"I'm sure you're right," she replied, because there didn't seem to be anything else she could say.

For a long moment he didn't say anything either or make a move for the door. She felt a brief hope that he might linger. Desperation fueled the feeling from a flicker to a full-blown inferno that swept through her.

Please stay.

It was such a ridiculous impulse she didn't even start to open her mouth to form the words. She didn't know this man. He didn't owe her anything, had already done more for her than most people would have bothered with, risking himself to come over and investigate. Asking for anything more would be too much.

But if he offered to do it himself…

He cleared his throat, not looking at her. "Okay, then. Good night."

Disappointment washed over her, the feeling too familiar to have much of an impact.

"Good night," she murmured.

He turned and walked out of the doorway. She listened to his heavy tread retreating, the sound of the front door closing, then to the empty silence echoing around her.

Apprehension clawed up her spine, prickling at the nape of her neck. She scanned the familiar space of her living room. The bookshelves filled from top to bottom on one wall. The comfortable, mismatched furniture, each piece personally chosen. She tried to tell herself that she was just as safe here as she'd been before she'd gone to bed. Maybe the officers were right. Maybe it had just been a bad dream.

Maybe…

But try as she might, she couldn't make herself believe any of it. The truth remained too vivid in her memory.

She unconsciously rubbed a hand over her belly. "Just you and me, little guy," she whispered, getting a kick against her palm in response. She couldn't be disappointed. It was how she'd expected it to be from the beginning. Just her and the baby.

She'd just never felt more alone than she did in that moment.

Or more afraid.

JAKE TRIED NOT TO FEEL guilty as he left his neighbor's house. She'd be fine. He'd talked to the cops himself, heard how they hadn't found anything. They'd seemed convinced she'd just had a bad dream, fueled by pregnancy hormones and a lack of sleep, and suffered an extreme reaction, firing at phantoms that weren't there. It made more sense than people breaking in to her house to attack her and leaving no trace of their presence behind.

Besides, he couldn't let himself get involved. A pregnant woman, with no sign of a father in the picture, was exactly the kind of woman he couldn't be around. She could grow attached too easily, come to depend on him. And he didn't have anything to offer her, or her kid.

His reasons made sense. They just didn't help erase the uneasy feeling that dogged him as he made his way back to his house.

She'd seemed so sure.

The look in her eyes tugged at him. When she'd stared at him over the gun. When they'd said their goodbyes moments ago. There'd been dark shadows beneath her eyes, a sign that she wasn't sleeping much, as she'd said. But her eyes had been clear and focused. Afraid.

And sure.

His gut clenched. Was it possible? The cops hadn't ventured much beyond the house, finding enough, or not enough, there to satisfy their belief that she'd imagined the whole thing. But then, there'd only been two of them, not really enough to do a thorough search. If they thought something had really happened, they might have called for more officers.

He stopped midway between his house and hers, considering. If someone had broken in to her house, they'd probably used the back door, the one he'd found unlocked. And they likely wouldn't have approached the house from the front and made their way to the back from there, in plain view of the street. They would have approached from behind.

He slowly turned in that direction. Several rows of trees lined the backs of their houses, forming a thick natural border with the homes on the other side. If someone had broken in to her house, the best way to approach—and to disappear—was through the trees, maybe even parking in the driveway of the house on the other side. He didn't know for sure, but he thought he remembered something about that house being empty. There would be no one to notice a vehicle arriving in the middle of the night and making use of its driveway.

Before he could question the impulse, he quickly moved back to his truck and retrieved a flashlight, then headed toward her backyard. It was a cloudy night, the moon only briefly and occasionally showing itself. The trees lay covered in darkness.

Switching on the light, he reached the edge of the woods behind her house and floated the beam across the ground. It didn't take him long to spot where the dirt had been disturbed. He crossed to the location and leaned closer, having no trouble identifying the marks.

Fresh footprints.

There was no reason they should be there. He couldn't picture his neighbor wandering around back here, leaving a cluster of footprints in shoes that looked too big to be hers. He didn't know why someone from the other side would be over here, even if the house was occupied. She might have had somebody working in her backyard, although he couldn't think of a reason they'd have been back this far. Not to mention the lawn didn't look like it had been mowed that week.

The prints were messy and indistinct, as though whoever had made them had been moving too quickly to leave much of an impression. Quickly, as if they were running from a pregnant woman with a gun?

Jake stared at the marks for a long moment, trying to convince himself he wasn't putting more stock in them than he should be. He had no reason to believe the impressions were connected to what had happened in her house tonight, and every reason to believe nothing had occurred.

Unless the intruders had been so careful to leave no trace of their presence that in their haste they overlooked this one, maybe counting on someone to discount it.

Unless he'd just missed them disappearing into the darkness as he came around the side of the house.

Unless he was already inside when they started their vehicle and drove away, if the sound had even been audible from the house.

Troubled by where his thoughts were leading him, he headed back to his house. He couldn't call the cops with something so inconclusive. They hadn't been inclined to believe her. He didn't think they'd be happy to be called back for this, if they did come back. He wondered if he should tell his neighbor. She might feel better knowing there could be reason to think she was right. Or she might be better off believing she wasn't instead of scaring her more.

Remembering the pills he'd dropped in the driveway, he started to the front of the house. He was almost there when he saw it. A car parked on the other side of the street, facing him. It sat just out of reach of the nearest streetlamps on either side, the faintest edges of their glow falling mere feet short of illuminating it. Instead, it was nearly invisible, a dark-colored sedan blending into the shadows. Still, he could see the single figure sitting in the front seat. And though he couldn't see the person's face, he suddenly knew without a doubt the driver was watching his neighbor's house.

He'd kept an eye on the street while they had waited for the police. The car hadn't been sitting there then.

Before he even thought about it, he started toward the vehicle.

He'd barely gone three steps when the

driver suddenly jerked forward in his seat. The engine roared to life. Jake started to pick up speed, muscles tensing in readiness to break out into a run. That damn pain shot down his leg, causing him to miss a step.

The sedan burst forward, leaping away from the curb and onto the street with a screech of its tires. He could do nothing but watch the car tear down the street, moving so fast he couldn't even get the license plate number.

Biting back a curse, he drew in a ragged breath. His shoulders slumped, seeming to weigh a thousand pounds each. He should be used to his body failing him by now. That didn't make it any easier to take.

He'd started to turn back toward his house when his gaze fell on his neighbor's. The curtain in the front window shifted slightly. She must have looked out to see what the noise was.

Grimacing, he changed direction, heading for her front door. The curtain shifted again. He knew she was watching.

By the time he made it to the door, she was already opening it a crack, peering out over the chain she kept fastened. "What's going on?"

"I don't think you were imagining anything."

Her eyes went wide. She slammed the

door shut. He heard the sound of the chain being withdrawn before she pulled the door open farther, the other hand braced protectively on her belly.

"What are you talking about?"

"There are fresh footprints by the trees behind your house. And that car was sitting across the street. I think the driver was watching your house."

She swallowed hard, looking as if she was going to be sick. "I knew it was real."

"They could come back. You shouldn't stay here."

"I have my gun."

"Next time they might, too."

He saw the words hit home. She gave her head a shaky nod. "You're right. I'll go to a hotel or something…."

Her voice wobbled just the slightest bit, enough that he felt it like a low blow in his gut. She looked scared and vulnerable, as if she wanted to look over her shoulder and make sure there was nobody there, waiting to jump out at her from inside her own home. Which suddenly seemed all too possible. Hell, how did either of them know somebody hadn't managed to break back in again? They had already managed to do it one time without leaving any trace.

As if she was thinking the same thing, her other hand went to her stomach, her arms stretching low. She looked as if she wanted to wrap her arms around herself.

No, not herself. Her baby.

Something painful hit him in the chest. Hard.

"You can stay with me."

The words came out on their own. Even as he said them, it seemed as if someone else was doing so. She looked just as surprised to hear them as he was, blinking up at him, her mouth falling open in a soft *O*.

"Just for tonight," he said roughly. "Until you figure out something else." Part of him wondered who he was saying it for, her or himself.

For a long moment she didn't say anything, staring at him, her eyes round and dazed. Then she nodded unsteadily. "Okay. Just for tonight. Let me get a few things."

She retreated back into the house. He watched her waddle away. He knew letting her stay with him was the right thing to do. She shouldn't be alone, not in her condition, not the way she was feeling. That didn't stop him from wanting to call her back and revoke the offer. The uneasiness had returned with a vengeance, clawing at his insides with greater ferocity, for entirely different reasons than before.

Because he'd seen something else, too, shimmering faintly in her big brown eyes.

Gratitude.

And he knew more than ever that he'd finally made the mistake he'd been avoiding from the first time he'd seen the pregnant woman next door.

Chapter Three

Jake held open the front door of his house for her. Sara stepped over the threshold, feeling almost as though she was stepping into a brand-new world.

A few hours ago, she'd never spoken to this man. Now she was spending what was left of the night in his home.

Of course, several things had happened to her in the past few hours that had never happened before. At least this one might be relatively positive.

It was only when she heard him close and lock the door behind them that she felt a moment's trepidation. She looked back at him, so big he nearly rendered the door superfluous, blocking the entire entryway himself. What if he was involved with the people who'd invaded her home and this was all part of some ploy to get her to his house where she'd be completely at his mercy? Or even if it wasn't, how did she know she was safe with this man? She didn't know anything about him. No one knew where she was. He could make her disappear and no one would ever know.

Then he turned around, allowing her to see the frown on his face. It hadn't shifted since he'd made the invitation. He'd made it clear the offer had been grudging at best, hardly the attitude to project if he'd wanted to give her a false sense of security.

Sara grimaced at her own foolish paranoia, forcing herself to relax slightly. She was letting the night's events go to her head.

Not to mention the fact that he'd barely looked at her since offering the invitation. Even now, he didn't, moving past her toward a hallway. "You can take my bed," he said gruffly.

"Oh, that's not necessary."

"It's the only one I've got. There's a spare bedroom, but I never bothered to put a bed in there." Whether or not he'd intended it, she didn't miss the unspoken message in his words. He hadn't expected, or wanted, guests. "I'm sure you need it more than I do."

"Honestly, I doubt I'll get any sleep the

rest of the night. And I sleep better sitting up these days anyway." At least without her body pillow, which she'd forgotten, not even thinking about sleeping. She had so much adrenaline pumping through her system it felt as if she'd never sleep again. "Just point me in the direction of a comfortable chair and I'll be set."

Looking unconvinced, he finally waved an arm toward the living room. Following the motion, she made her way to a chair a few feet away. The room was barely furnished. If she hadn't known better, she would have thought he'd just moved in that day. A flatscreen TV was installed on one wall directly in front of the chair. Some weights, an exercise mat and a workout bench were clustered in one corner. A card table set up beside the chair bore a few magazines. All sports-related, she noted, as she lowered herself into the seat.

Folding his arms over his chest, he leaned a shoulder against the wall. She realized with a start that the chair she'd gravitated toward was the only seat in the living room other than the bench. Boy, this place really wasn't intended to accommodate guests in any way.

"Do you want to call the police?" he asked.

"And tell them what? There was a car sitting outside my house? I'm sure they'll want to rush right over for that, especially since they didn't believe me before." She wiped a hand across her forehead. "I'll go to the police station in the morning. Hopefully I'll find somebody who might be more willing to believe me."

"I'll go with you." She must have seemed surprised, because he shrugged his free shoulder. "I'm the one who saw the car, right?"

"Of course." This time they couldn't claim she'd imagined it. At the very least, it would have to be a shared delusion. "It's weird, though."

"What?"

"If whoever was in the car was one of the same people who broke in to my house, why would he park right across the street, for everyone to see after going to all the trouble of coming through the backyard the first time?"

"Could be they were just checking to make sure the coast was clear. As soon as they were sure the police were gone, they'd go around back and try again."

"Maybe," she said, unable to keep the doubt from her voice. It still felt as if something wasn't adding up. "How many people were in the car?"

"It was dark. I could only see the driver."

"There were three people in my house. I'm sure of it."

"The big question is how they got inside in the first place."

"I don't know. The police said the locks hadn't been tampered with, and I know I locked the back door."

"I noticed you don't have a security system."

"It never seemed necessary. This is supposed to be a safe community. It's one reason I moved here. I'm sure you don't have one, either." He signaled his agreement with a terse jerk of his head. "Logically, the only way they could have gotten in was with a key. But I've never given one to anybody."

"Do you have one hidden somewhere around the house in case you get locked out?"

"No."

"Maybe they stole yours somehow and made a copy without your knowledge."

Sara suppressed a shudder. He'd reached the same conclusion she had. "That would mean they put some forethought into this, actually planned it for some time before going through with it. But who would do that? And why?"

"You really don't know why anyone would attack you?"

She gave her head a vigorous shake. "No."

He nodded at her belly. "What about the father?"

"He's not in the picture."

Something in her tone must have grabbed his suspicions, because his gaze sharpened. "How 'not in the picture' is he?"

"Completely. He doesn't even know about the baby."

"Because you didn't tell him?" She nodded. "What if he found out on his own? He might not have been too happy to find out you kept it a secret."

"No, it's not like that—" Sara swallowed a sigh. She'd known it would likely come to this, but had still held out some small hope that she could avoid the question. And the answer. She'd almost been relieved when the police hadn't bothered asking. Their lack of belief in her intruders had had that benefit at least.

For eight and a half months she hadn't told a single person. She'd deftly avoided her doctor's questions, and there hadn't been anyone else to tell. That was one good thing about her solitary existence. It made it easier to avoid embarrassing questions.

That seemed less likely to be the case if she managed to convince the police to believe her. Like Jake, they would probably want to know more about the circumstances that led to her present state. If she did have to tell, maybe it wouldn't be so bad to have a practice run at it with someone who didn't really care either way.

She took a breath. "I don't know who he is."

To his credit, Jake didn't even blink. He simply gave a solemn nod in response. "Well, if you give the cops the names of the potential fathers, they can probably track them down and see where they might have been tonight."

Another, deeper, breath. "That's not what I meant. I know when and with whom I got pregnant. I just don't know his name. It was a one-time thing."

"And you didn't get his name."

It was probably her imagination, but she thought she heard the first trace of judgment in his tone. She stared him straight in the eye and tried to fight the heat she felt rising in her cheeks. "He said his name was Mark."

"No last name?"

"I assume he has one. He just didn't share it with me."

"You didn't ask?"

"No."

"Did you tell him your full name?"

"No, just my first."

"Does he know where you live?"

"I didn't tell him, no."

"Still, it's not a big town. If he saw you on the street or something…"

"It happened in the city."

"So there's no reason to believe he has any idea where to find you, or that you're pregnant."

"That's right. Like I said, he's not involved."

"And there's nobody else you can think of who might have reason to break into your house and attack you?"

"No."

Clearly stumped, he shook his head. "Then I don't know. Hopefully the police can figure it out." He pushed away from the door frame. "I should let you rest."

"And I'm sure I've kept you up longer than you intended."

He nodded shortly, which she took to be a sign of agreement. "Feel free to use the TV. Yell if you need anything. I'll leave the door open in case you do."

"Okay."

With another tight nod, he turned away

and stalked toward the hallway. Not for the first time, she noticed the slight hitch in his step, the way he slightly favored his left leg over the right. She'd wondered about its cause, but wasn't about to ask. It really wasn't any of her business.

She watched his broad back receding. He was almost out of sight when she felt the outburst pressing against her throat. She couldn't hold it back.

"Jake?"

It was the first time she'd said his name, and she immediately realized they hadn't established if they were on a first-name basis. For his part, he hadn't called her anything besides the "lady" he'd used when he'd entered her house. Another way of maintaining some semblance of distance between them, she supposed. She wondered if he'd take offense at her familiarity.

He stopped, his shoulders tensing. He didn't look back.

"Thank you," she said, her voice thick, "for—"

"Don't mention it."

The words were tossed over his shoulder without a glance back. As soon as they were out, he started moving again, not waiting for a response. Seconds later he disappeared into the bedroom. As he'd said, he left the door open. She waited for a light to come on. It didn't. He must have decided not to bother.

She settled back in the chair, trying not to take his reaction for the rejection it was. He was simply reminding her of a truth she'd be better off remembering. He wasn't her friend. He was barely an acquaintance. Her neighbor, nothing more.

For tonight, though, it was enough. And she had more important things to worry about in the morning.

The reminder brought back everything that had happened that night. He'd left all the lights in the living room on for her. She should have felt safe. But the room opened onto the kitchen, and when she glanced to her right, she had a clear view of both the windows over the sink and in the back door. And once she saw them, she couldn't look away.

The windows gaped with darkness. There was no light on outside the back door. The backyard was out there, and beyond it, the trees. Where he'd found footprints.

Anyone could be out there.

Anyone might be.

Eyes wide, Sara swallowed the hard lump that formed in her throat. Rubbing a hand over her belly, she stared at the windows, into the darkness, and desperately wished for morning to come.

Chapter Four

Sara didn't know how she managed to get any sleep during the endless night. She only knew that she had, when she found herself prodded awake by a familiar urge.

Sunlight filtered in through the windows she'd stared at for so long. It was morning. Slowly hoisting herself from the chair, she moved toward the hallway, already having located the bathroom during an earlier trip in the middle of the night.

She'd just reached the corridor when her neighbor stepped through the still open doorway of his bedroom.

Her drowsiness vanished in an instant, her eyes going wide. Like her, he'd obviously just gotten up. He was tousle-haired and bare-chested, dressed only in a pair of skimpy shorts that didn't even stretch halfway to his knees and hardly managed to contain his thighs. She tried to avoid looking at the impressive bulge between them. God knew there was plenty else to look at.

She'd known he was muscular; that was apparent even when he was dressed. It was something else entirely to see him without clothes, to see just how hard and toned his body was. There wasn't a stray ounce of fat anywhere, only firm skin stretched over taut muscle. His arms were massive, as big around as his thighs.

A tremor of awareness, so unexpected, so unfamiliar, quaked through her, rumbling upward from the pit of her stomach.

He detected her presence a moment after she spotted him, coming to a stop just outside his bedroom. He dragged a hand over his face, the eyes narrowed with sleepiness only widening the slightest bit. "'Morning," he said, his voice a hoarse rumble.

"Good morning," she murmured. "I was just…" She waved a hand toward the bathroom.

He nodded. "Go ahead." Before she could respond, he ducked back into his bedroom.

When she finally emerged from the bathroom, she shuffled back into the living room. He was standing at the front window, pulling a curtain back slightly with one finger and peering out. He'd pulled a T-shirt on, an impossibly large swath of cloth covering the wide expanse of his back, but hadn't bothered with pants. He was still wearing those impossibly short shorts.

An ache started low in her belly as her gaze tracked down the curve of his back to the outline of his buttocks and those substantial thighs, firm as barrels and lightly dusted with dark hair—

She jerked her eyes up, heat filling her cheeks, even though his back was turned and there was no way he could see her. There wasn't nearly enough of the window exposed for him to see her reflected in it. That didn't prevent her embarrassment. What was she doing?

Hormones, she thought. She was pregnant and horny. There was certainly no denying it as she couldn't quite prevent her gaze from slipping lower again, a rush of adrenaline surging through her.

"The car's back."

Her thoughts were so distracted that it took a moment for the words to sink in. "Hmm?"

"I can't tell if it's the same one, but I'd bet anything it is. It's sitting in damn near the same spot it was last night."

What he was saying finally managed to

break through the heady rush of hormones, killing the delicious thrill.

The car. Last night.

All her tension, all the fear that she'd only managed to shake came rushing back. She frowned, her stomach clenching.

The reason he was only pulling back the curtain a little bit finally hit her. He didn't want whoever was out there to know he was watching.

The same way that person was watching them.

Or was he? Did he know she was at Jake's, or was he still watching her house?

Moving as quickly as she could, Sara crossed the room to his side. "Can you see the license plate?"

"No. It's too bright. The sun's hitting it just right and making it too hard to see."

He looked down, then started, as if surprised to see her there. A flicker of…something slid along her nerve endings. She hadn't realized just how close she'd come to him, focused solely on what he was looking at. She was standing right next to him, as close as they could possibly be without touching. Much closer than common courtesy dictated. She should step back.

Instead, she could only stare up into his eyes, feeling his closeness, unable to move.

Gray, she thought distantly. His eyes were gray. The color of storm clouds on a rainy day.

Abruptly the connection was broken. It was he who stepped back, away from her, letting the curtain fall. A flash of some unreadable emotion passed over those eyes she now knew were gray. He frowned, dropping his gaze. "Take a look."

Strangely, inexplicably shaken, she slid over partly into the space he'd vacated and pushed the curtain ever so slightly to the side.

The bright morning sunlight blinded her for a moment. It took a few seconds for her vision to clear. Gradually the vehicle came into focus. It was as he'd said. There was a black sedan parked on the other side of the street, slightly down from her house, no doubt offering a good view of it without being right out front. The light bounced off the body and windows, making it impossible to see who was inside.

"I don't suppose it would do any good to try and confront him," she said.

"I'd bet anything he'd drive away as soon as he saw me coming."

She shot him a glance. "You? I think I'd like to have a word with him to find out why the hell he's watching my house."

Jake stared down at her. So gradually she didn't realize it was happening at first, a hint of wry humor entered his gaze, his eyes crinkling at the corners, his mouth twitching. "You really think you could move fast enough to catch him?"

"Maybe not," she conceded. "But I wouldn't mind trying."

He continued looking at her, that unfamiliar glint in his eyes, that barely discernible smile on his lips.

A strange flutter in her belly, she turned back to the window. Almost as soon as she did, she heard the sound of an engine starting. Moments later the car pulled away from the curb.

"He's leaving."

Beside her, she felt Jake moving away. She tried to read the license plate, only to be distracted when the driver's door came into view. He must have had the window down, because it was sliding upward as he moved past, the raised glass reflecting the sunlight, cutting him off from view. She'd seen only enough to confirm her suspicion that it was probably a man.

In the back of her mind she registered the sound of the front door opening. When the car was gone, she turned to see Jake stepping back inside the house. He quickly moved to the table, grabbed a pen and jotted something down.

"I got the make and license plate number. Did you see him?" Jake asked.

Sara shook her head, letting the curtain drop. "No. He rolled up his window."

"I guess it's time to try the police again. Let me get dressed and we can go."

He moved away without waiting for her response, heading down the hall. Her eyes helplessly, hungrily tracked every motion, every shift of his shoulders, every flex of his buttocks and thighs, until he disappeared into the bedroom.

Once he was out of view she gave herself a shake. *Hormones,* she thought again on a sigh. She hadn't been this aware of a man since… Well, since the night that landed her in her current condition.

And if she needed a reminder of exactly why she needed to get a grip, that certainly did it.

"AND THEN IT DROVE AWAY," Sara said, even as she wondered why she was bothering. Detective Baxter wasn't taking her seriously.

Worse, he was barely paying attention to her. Other than a cursory glance in her direction while she was speaking to signal he was supposedly listening, his gaze kept drifting back to Jake, seated beside her in front of the detective's desk.

Having reached the end of her patience, she was about to say something about it when Baxter shot upright in his chair. He snapped his fingers and grinned broadly at Jake.

"Football. Linebacker, right?"

He might as well have started speaking gibberish. Bewildered, Sara glanced at Jake to see if he knew what the man was talking about.

From the tightness that gripped his features, he did. His lips thinned. "Right."

"I knew you looked familiar. You got hurt last year."

"Yeah."

"I saw that game. Man, that injury looked brutal."

Jake's eyes narrowed. "It was."

"You know, the local high school team's going to start practice up again pretty soon. I'm sure they'd love it if you could talk to them."

"Sorry. I'm not sure how much longer I'll be around, with the season starting up and all."

The detective's eyebrows shot sky-high. "You looking to get back in the game?"

"It's a possibility."

"I heard your career was over."

"We'll see."

Based on his curt, mostly monosyllabic answers, Sara thought it was obvious Jake didn't want to talk about it. The detective still leaned forward expectantly, as though he expected Jake to elaborate.

Jake stared back. He didn't say a word.

When the silence went on too long, Sara cleared her throat.

Baxter glanced at her, annoyance flickering across his face before his expression regained its condescending coolness.

"Ms. Carson, I'll take down your report, but I'm not sure what else I can do. There's still no sign anybody was in your house. All you've given me is some footprints that could have been left there anytime and a car that could have been there for any reason."

Sara tried to swallow her rising anger in the face of the man's condescension. Evidently that particular trait was a common one in the local police department. "A car that took off as soon as its driver realized it was spotted."

"No offense, but a lot of people might be intimidated seeing this guy coming at them in the dark, even if they're not doing anything wrong." He grinned at Jake.

Jake stared back, unimpressed.

Baxter's grin quickly died. He straightened in his seat. "We also had a car drive by a couple of times as promised and they didn't see anything suspicious."

"Because whoever was out there had already been scared off. Maybe for a second time, if it was the same people who broke in to my house in the first place."

The detective sighed. "Look, I'll run the plate and see if anything suspicious comes up. If something else happens, let us know. Other than that, there's not much I can do."

Recognizing the finality in both his words and his tone, and figuring she'd wasted enough of her time with this man, Sara forced herself to offer a cordial "Thank you for your time." She would have loved to say something more cutting, but there was still the chance she might need this man's help, if she ever managed to convince him there was something he could help her with.

More than ready to get out of there, she started the arduous process of getting to her feet. She'd barely moved before Jake was standing before her, offering his hand. With a grateful smile, she accepted the hand and let him help her up, doing her best to ignore the jolt that shot up her arm when his large, warm fingers closed around hers and threatened to swallow them whole.

When they finally stepped outside the police station, she heaved a sigh, pleased to be out of there, if not about anything else. "Well, that was a waste of time. I'm sorry you came all the way down here for nothing."

"We had to try, at any rate."

"Too bad all we accomplished was giving Baxter a thrill for the day." She glanced up at him, her eyebrows raised. "I didn't know you were a celebrity."

His expression hardened. "I'm not."

Moving slowly, they started toward his truck, which was parked at the curb just down the block. "People know who you are. I'm pretty sure that makes you a celebrity."

"Depends who the people are. You didn't know who I was."

She grimaced apologetically. "I'm sorry. I don't follow sports."

"A lot of people don't. Even a lot of people who do wouldn't be able to pick me out of a lineup. Not much of a celebrity. I'm fine with that."

And he was, she thought, remembering how uncomfortable he'd been when the detective recognized him. That would teach her to stereotype. She would have assumed a professional athlete would be flashier, more of a glory hound. Or maybe he'd simply grown beyond that since it appeared his glory days were behind him.

"Is it true what he said?" she asked carefully. "You were injured?"

"Yeah."

"How bad was it?"

"Blew out my knee. Had surgery to put it together again, but I'm still trying to get back to where I was."

"I'm sorry."

"It is what it is," he said, clear dismissal in his tone. They'd reached the truck. Jake pulled the passenger door open for her.

After helping her get in, he closed the door and moved around to his side. "What do you want to do now?" he asked.

"Do you remember that license plate number?"

"Sure."

She reached into her purse and pulled out her cell phone. "I'll run it myself. Give it to me."

Jake was so surprised that he could only obey, watching as she quickly typed a text message and hit Send.

She shoved the phone back into her purse. "She'll get back to me ASAP."

"You have somebody who can run license plates for you?"

She grinned. "Yep. Who needs the cops, anyway?"

For a moment he was struck dumb and could only stare into that big, beautiful smile, so different from anything he'd ever seen or expected to see on her face. He'd thought she was pretty before. The smile only confirmed it. Her whole face seemed to light up with it.

And then the smile was fading, her eyes flickering uncertainly, her self-consciousness clear. "What?"

He cleared his throat, which had suddenly gone dry, and pushed his key into the ignition. "Nothing. Why didn't you contact her earlier?"

"It didn't seem worth the trouble if we were coming to see the police, anyway. I guess I was hoping they would do their jobs and I wouldn't have to bother."

Starting the engine, he smoothly pulled away from the curb. "So who is this person? Somebody with the state?"

"No, someone who does research for me with resources she says I'm probably better off not knowing about. I have a feeling she's right about that. All that matters is she can find out just about anything I need."

"Research?" he echoed. "Maybe I should be asking what *you* do."

She hesitated and lowered her eyes, her sudden tension clear. "I'm a writer."

"What do you write?"

Another hesitation. "Books."

"Anything I'd have heard of?"

"It's kind of private."

"More private than what you told me last night?"

She sighed and said nothing. For a moment he wasn't sure she was going to respond. "You heard of Brock Marshall?"

It took him a few seconds to make the connection. Brock Marshall was the main character in a series of action thrillers, a globe-trotting mercenary whose sex-filled, überviolent escapades had slowly developed a loyal audience. The fourth one had come out a couple months ago and quickly become the biggest one yet, making a bunch of bestseller lists. There was even talk of a movie being developed, except none of the current stock of Hollywood pretty boys could live up to the embodiment of raw masculinity that Marshall represented. Jake had read a couple of the books himself and knew plenty of guys who loved them, even among men who didn't do much reading beyond the *Sports Illustrated* swimsuit issue. The books were written by—

His train of thought came to a screeching halt. He whipped his head toward her in disbelief. "*You're* S.J. Carson?"

Her eyes were downcast and there was a tightness in her expression, as if she was bracing herself for his reaction. "I see you have heard of him."

He quickly returned his attention to the road. "Sure." S.J. Carson was the credited author of the Brock Marshall books. The book jacket didn't say much about the author, just that he was a world traveler working on his next book or something.

Except now that Jake thought about it, the short one-line bio didn't exactly say Carson was a he. That just seemed to be the natural assumption. Given the sense of authenticity surrounding the militaristic and espionage elements, the author seemed likely to be someone with military experience, obviously well-traveled, perhaps presenting a highly exaggerated, idealized version of himself.

Certainly not a young woman with a shy smile and retreating gaze.

A burst of surprised laughter rose in his throat.

Until he glanced over and saw the expression on her face.

She grimaced at him, her gaze almost apologetic. "Not what you were expecting, am I?"

"No," he said honestly. "I can't say that you are."

"I figured. Somehow I doubt when people imagine S.J. Carson, I'm what they would picture."

"That's what you were going for, right? By using your initials instead of your real name?"

"My publisher thought it would sell better if we were a little circumspect about my identity. It didn't seem likely anyone would want to read an action novel about a soldier of fortune if they knew it was written by a chubby twenty-three-year-old girl who'd never been out of the country." She shrugged a shoulder. "I expected it. I mean, J.K. Rowling was asked to use her initials so boys wouldn't be turned off reading the Harry Potter books."

"But eventually it came out that she was a woman, and it wasn't a problem."

"So it turned out little boys are more accepting than big ones. Research shows a lot of men won't read books written by women, especially with male protagonists, as though they'll be too girly and full of people talking about their feelings."

"That sure doesn't sound like any of your books."

A faint hint of her earlier grin returned. "I've found sudden explosions and unexpected shootings are good ways to break up an overly emotional moment."

"So prove them wrong. Everybody knows your books now."

She shrugged. "I don't know that it's worth the risk. If a bunch of readers decide they don't want to read the books because I'm the one writing them, what then? You can't unring a bell. Besides, I'm about as interested in being a celebrity as you are. I'd rather my readers like my stories without worrying about whether they like me." A sad, almost defeated note climbed into her voice as she said the final words, as though she'd already decided that they wouldn't.

He glanced at her and frowned.

"Twenty-three, huh?"

"I wrote the first book in college. While all the other English majors were working on their depressing tomes about how terrible life is, I wanted to write something where the good guys win and everything ends well."

"You're an optimist," he said, unable to keep it from sounding like an insult.

A dry laugh burst from her throat. "Hardly. I think the reason we need happy endings in fiction is because they're so hard to find in real life."

"Why Brock Marshall? Why not write about a woman?"

"Why? Because women are only supposed to write about women?"

From the sudden sharpness in her tone, he'd hit a nerve. "No. Just wondering."

As if realizing her overreaction, she sent him an apologetic glance. "Because the books are as much an escape for me as they are for the reader. That wouldn't be the case if I was writing about someone like me. I wanted to write about someone as far from me as possible."

"I don't know if that's true. You didn't have any trouble with that gun last night. Seems like something Brock Marshall would do."

"Chalk it up to research," she said with a soft smile, the sight of it sending another twinge through his chest. "I needed to know how to shoot a gun to write about it, so I took a few lessons at the firing range. Then it seemed like a good thing to have on hand for protection."

"Guess you proved that one true."

"Trust me, I would have rather not had the opportunity."

Her cell phone must have given some indication she had a new message, because she suddenly reached into her bag and pulled it out. "That was fast." She hit a few buttons and read the screen. "The car is registered to a Roger Halloran of Boston."

"Someone you know?"

"I've never heard of him," she murmured, typing a return message. "I'll ask Raven to see what she can dig up for me, and I'll do a search online when I get home."

She was just putting the phone away again when he pulled onto their street. As their houses—or maybe just hers—came into view, he felt her tense beside him. He understood the instinct. She might have a lead on whoever had attacked her, but hadn't accomplished much in terms of preventing it from happening again. The prospect of going home couldn't hold much appeal for her.

"You should change your locks," he told her. "Do you know a locksmith around here?"

"No, but I'm sure I can look one up."

"I can change them for you. Let's go back into town and stop by the hardware store." Frankly, he should have thought of it before.

"You don't have to do that. Besides, I'm not entirely sure I want to stay at the house right now." She shook her head, rubbing a hand over her belly anxiously. "I keep thinking that maybe I should get a room somewhere, but for how long? I can't hide forever, and without knowing why someone broke in or why they're watching me, I have no idea how long I'd have to stay away before they give up. If they do."

He had to agree with her assessment. Somebody who'd gone to all this trouble wasn't going to give up until they had what they wanted. A hotel room in the city might be safer, but they could track her down there.

He stopped the truck in front of his house, but didn't pull into the driveway. "And there's nobody you can stay with? A friend?"

"No."

"Family?"

Her lips thinned. "I don't have any."

"What about somebody who helps you with the baby? Aren't you supposed to have a person to help you breathe or something when the time comes?"

She shifted uncomfortably in her seat. "Ideally, but I don't. I bought an instructional video and watched a few others online to learn what I'm supposed to do. I figure it won't be too hard to do by myself. I've been breathing on my own for twenty-nine years now." She tried for a weak smile that fell short.

"How long have you lived around here anyway?"

The redness in her face deepened. "Five years," she practically whispered.

"And you don't know anybody?"

"I tend to keep to myself," she mumbled.

It wasn't as if he could argue with that. He knew that much from personal experience.

"Look," she said quickly, as though figuring the statement demanded an explanation. "The thing is, I've never been very good at meeting people and making friends. I get nervous and I don't know what to say, and it's embarrassing for everyone involved. I'm just not good at talking to people and making conversation."

"You can't be that bad. Brock Marshall always has a clever line."

"I'm not Brock Marshall," she pointed out, a trace of embarrassment or maybe apology in her tone. "Besides, there's a difference between making conversation and making up conversation. Dialogue's a lot easier when you get to do both sides of the discussion."

"You're doing okay now."

She frowned and appeared to consider the comment. "I guess so," she said, sounding surprised to realize he was right.

He frowned, too, as it occurred to him that he could say the same for himself. She wasn't the only one who considered herself not much of a talker. He'd said more to this woman in less than twenty-four hours than he had in months to anyone who wasn't a medical professional. Then again, they'd had a lot to talk about. Coming up with conversation the past few hours hadn't exactly been tough.

He stared at her house through the windshield. Leaving her there by herself seemed even more wrong that it had last night. At the same time, the idea of her alone, far from home, made his stomach clench.

This time the words didn't come as quite a surprise. "You can stay with me until you figure it out."

"That's really generous, Jake, and I appreciate the offer, I really do. But I don't want to impose on you any more than I already have."

He fought the guilt her words inspired, knowing he'd made it clear he hadn't really wanted her in his house, even as he realized that was no longer entirely true.

"I wouldn't offer if I didn't mean it. Besides, you shouldn't be alone."

"I have my gun."

"And you're going to have to sleep sometime, no matter where you go. Unless you want to hire a bodyguard or something." Actually, that didn't sound half bad. She could use someone to watch over her until she knew what was going on. Someone who was more of an expert than he was. Someone to take over this strange responsibility he felt for her.

"I don't know if I could afford one, or for how long." He must have looked surprised that S.J. Carson would have to take money into consideration, because she explained, "The books are doing well, but I'm far from rich. Between my student loans and buying my house and my car, not to mention baby expenses, I've had plenty of bills to pay over the past few years. I have some money in the bank I've been saving for when the baby arrives, but I'd rather not tap into it unless absolutely necessary."

"So stay. We'll figure this out."

She eyed him for a long moment. This time there was none of the gratitude he thought he'd detected the night before. There was merely uncertainty, along with a distinct hint of wariness.

Something that felt strangely like shame

washed over him. In his attempt to ward off her gratitude, he'd made it clear that any thankfulness was unwanted and his assistance was begrudging, giving her no reason to agree to any more of it.

The unfamiliar word surged from his throat, damn near sticking at the last moment before bursting past his lips. "Please," he said, his voice ragged, sounding as unused to saying it as it was. "Stay. Let me help you."

Her eyes widened with surprise. She swallowed. "Okay," she said softly, tentatively. "Thank you."

He couldn't have described the inexplicable relief he felt at hearing her agree. Like many other emotions, it was best left unexamined.

He didn't say anything else, acknowledging her answer with a tight nod, and pulled the truck into the driveway.

Chapter Five

"I found something."

After stopping by her house long enough to grab her laptop and some clothes, they'd returned to his house and she'd immediately jumped online, setting up her computer on the card table. Keeping her eyes on the screen, Sara sensed rather than saw Jake's approach. "What is it?" he asked.

"Roger Halloran is mentioned in a bunch of news stories from Boston about a year ago. If it's the same man, he's a police officer whose teenage daughter disappeared last August." Sara swallowed. "And here's the interesting part. She was pregnant. Only a few months—I doubt she was even showing—but definitely pregnant. The media really played up that angle. Considering how stories about missing pregnant women and missing teenagers go over, I'm not surprised. I was deep in final revisions on a book at the time, which must be how I missed hearing about it."

Jake didn't say anything for a moment. She could sense him trying to absorb the information much as she was. The detail seemed too significant not to mean something.

"Did they find her?"

"Not that I can tell. There's no mention of her being found. It looks like she's still missing."

"And now her father's watching you. It's probably not a coincidence."

"No, I don't think so, either. I just don't know what the connection could be. I didn't know her."

"Maybe you reminded him of his daughter and he became fixated on you. Is there a picture? Did she look anything like you?"

"Not at all." Sara turned the laptop so he could see. Tricia Halloran had been blond, petite and just sixteen. Her features were more delicate and she'd been half a foot shorter than Sara.

"Strange," he murmured. "Maybe the pregnancy was enough to get his attention."

"The only way to know is to ask the man himself, but he'd drive away before we had the chance."

"Then maybe we shouldn't give him the opportunity to drive away."

She frowned up at him. "Should we call the police?"

"I still don't think they'll be in any rush to come over, do you? And even if they do come and question the guy, they probably won't get anything out of him. I'm sure he'd have a perfectly good explanation for why he was there."

"So what do you want to do?"

He cocked a brow, the corner of his mouth curling in the beginning of a grin. Her heart did a peculiar jump in her chest. "I'll go get him, and I won't give him a chance to see me."

"THE CAR IS BACK." Adrenaline surging, Jake stepped away from the window. "It's showtime."

Sara stopped the nervous pacing she'd been doing for the past half hour, her hands braced behind her back as she slowly toddled across the living room, and looked at him head-on. She dropped her hands to her sides, her shoulders tensing. "Are you sure you want to do this?"

"Don't you want to know why he's out there?"

"Yeah, I do."

"Then let's find out. Can I have your gun?" He'd already explained the plan and told her that he'd need to borrow her weapon for this.

"Right." Padding across the room, she pulled the pistol out of her bag and handed it to him.

He quickly checked it over, familiarizing himself with it. It had been a while since he'd handled a firearm, and he was more experienced with a hunting rifle than a handgun, but he doubted he'd have any problems. If all went well, he wouldn't even have to use it.

Keeping it in his hand, he headed for the back door. "See you in a few."

He was about to open it when she called out. "Jake."

He glanced back.

She stood there, uncertainty written across her face. "Be careful."

The worry in her eyes, the depth of feeling in those hoarsely whispered words, touched something deep inside him and he hesitated for a moment. It should have been nothing more than a rote phrase, something to say just to be said.

Coming from her, it was more than that. She wasn't just saying it. She really meant it.

She truly didn't want anything to happen

to him, in a way that went beyond common courtesy. She cared, and that was exactly what he didn't want. At least it was what he shouldn't want. But damned if he could remember the last time anyone had bothered to care about what happened to him on a level like this woman was displaying. And damned if he didn't feel a little off balance as a result.

He cleared his throat. "I will." Forcing his off-kilter emotions aside, he slipped out the door and into the darkened backyard.

Night had fallen just over an hour ago. Jake quickly moved past Sara's house and the one next to it, finally rounding the third one down from his. Thankfully the lights were off, the neighbors not home to see him skulking around their house. He paused at the front, peering around the corner to confirm he was now behind the car.

Staying in the shadows, he darted across the street, winding up in the dark space between two streetlights. The vehicle sat about fifty yards ahead. He could see the driver's reflection in the side mirror. Halloran's attention remained fixed on the house. He didn't appear to have noticed Jake.

The driver's window was open, no doubt so he'd have a better chance of hearing any sounds that might come from the house, not to mention keeping cool in the August heat. Jake approached carefully, moving on the balls of his feet, trying not to make a sound. Only when he was within a few yards of the car did he move faster, rushing toward the door before the driver could react and start the engine.

Jake stepped up to the window and aimed the gun directly in the man's face. Sure enough, his right hand was reaching for the ignition. "Hands up."

Clenching his jaw, Halloran slowly raised his hands, showing his palms. His expression said he knew he was defeated, and didn't like it one bit.

"Roger Halloran?" Jake phrased it as a question, even though there was none in his mind. The man matched the picture Sara's researcher had sent.

"How'd you know my name?"

"We ran your license plate." The man swore, reflecting how he felt about that news. "Get out of the car."

"Why?"

"I've got a lady who'd like a word with you."

Halloran hesitated. "The folder on the front seat. I should get it."

Jake narrowed his gaze in suspicion. "Why?"

The man met his stare, his eyes cold and lifeless. "Because you're going to want to see what's inside."

Jake shifted to his left until the passenger seat came into view. He flicked a quick glance at it, not willing to take his eyes off Halloran for long. A thick folder crammed with papers lay there. No weapon of any kind appeared to be under or next to it.

"All right. Slowly," he ordered when Halloran started to reach for the folder a little too quickly for his liking. Halloran complied, picking up the file with his right hand and holding it up in front of him.

Jake pulled the door open with his free hand and gave a quick jerk of his head.

"Now move."

SARA PEERED THROUGH the curtains in the front window and watched the two men approach the house. Halloran was in the lead, with Jake so close behind that he was obviously holding the gun on the man.

She stared at the newcomer's face as they came nearer. His weathered features were hard as granite, his stare cold and unblinking. A shudder rolled through her. She had no trouble believing this man would try to hurt her.

When they reached the front path, she moved to the door and pulled it open, then stepped backward. Moments later, Halloran entered the doorway without pausing on the threshold.

"Halloran, I think you know Sara Carson," Jake said.

The man signaled his agreement by lifting his head in a terse nod. His eyes barely connected with hers, an unreadable emotion in them, before skimming down her body, coming to land on her stomach.

Almost reflexively, Sara moved a hand to her belly, wishing she could so easily block the force of the man's cold stare.

Jake kicked the door shut behind them. Keeping the gun on Halloran, he crossed to the workout bench in the corner of the room and dragged it in front of the card table with one hand. The end he was holding dropped to the carpet with a thud. "Take a seat," he told Halloran.

For a moment it looked as if the man might refuse the order. He finally lowered himself onto the bench, resistance etched in every tense line of his body.

Sara eased herself into the chair across

from him, looking him straight in the eye even as every instinct wanted to look away from that eerie intensity in his gaze. "You've been watching me, haven't you? I'd like to know why."

By way of answer, he opened the folder and pulled out a photograph, setting it on the table in front of her. "I believe you know this man."

Frowning, she automatically glanced down.

Her breath caught in her throat.

Yes, she did know that man. Intimately. Even if she'd only known him for one night.

It was Mark.

The man who'd fathered her baby.

For the first few weeks after that night, his face had remained vivid in her mind. But over time the image had faded, leaving behind only vague impressions of his features. Only the memory of how he'd made her feel had stuck with her. She'd been increasingly sad about it, trying to remember his face with greater desperation every day, needing that sole link to her child's father.

One glance was all it took to restore her memory and fill in all the details that time had erased. He was beautiful. It was the first thing that had popped into her head when she'd first seen him and the impression held up now.

Even seeing his picture made her heart beat a little faster. Short blond hair. Intense, deep blue eyes. A lean, chiseled face. And his mouth… She'd never really noticed men's mouths before, but there was something about his—his lips so perfectly formed, soft and supple, yet undeniably masculine. She could have stared at his mouth alone for hours.

Halloran's voice cut into her thoughts. "You recognize him, don't you?"

"Yes," she said over the hard knot in her throat. "How did you know that?"

"I'd been tailing him for a while before you two hooked up."

"Why?"

He reached back into his folder, this time producing a small stack of several photographs he began to line up on the table above the one of Mark. The face of a teenage girl smiled up from each one.

"Eve Riordan. Lauren Gates. Jenny Kearney. Madison Hatch." He paused before completing the lineup with the final photograph. "Tricia," he choked out, voice clogged with emotion.

"Halloran," Sara finished for him. "Your daughter."

He nodded tersely. "Five teenage girls

who disappeared and haven't been found or heard from since."

A whisper of unease slid down her spine. "You think they're connected?"

"I know they are. They all had some other things in common. All of them were a few months pregnant when they disappeared." He stabbed a finger at the picture of Mark. "And they all knew this man. Mark Williams."

Williams. So that was his surname, at last. The revelation barely sank in, overshadowed by the rest of his statement. "How did they know him?"

"He worked as a counselor at the Great Start Youth Center in the city. That's another connection between them. After the third girl disappeared, the cops finally figured they'd all been to the center. It's one of those places with after-school programs for teens, counseling, a shelter for homeless kids and runaways, that kind of thing."

"And you think he was involved in their disappearances?"

"I know it."

"How? I'm sure he's not the only person who worked there."

"No. But he's the only one with a family history."

"What do you mean?"

"Williams wasn't his real name. He was born Mark William Kendall. He changed it when he turned eighteen, probably to avoid any connection with his past."

"His past?"

"Twenty-five years ago his mother, Marilyn Kendall, was arrested for running an illegal adoption ring in New Hampshire. She would convince young pregnant girls to give their babies up for adoption, then sell them at a premium to the highest bidder. She only ran into trouble when one of the girls came back wanting her baby. Evidently the girl wouldn't let it go and threatened to go the police. The Kendall woman snapped and killed her in a fit of rage. They don't think she was the only one, either, but that's when her operation started to fall apart, until the whole business came out. She went to prison, where she died seven years ago. That's where the story would have ended, except that Junior decided to get into the family business."

Sara frowned, trying to wrap her mind around the flood of information. "Wait a minute. You think he kidnapped these girls to sell their babies?"

"Exactly. I think Junior improved on his

mother's process. Marilyn Kendall got caught because a mother wanted her baby back. So Junior decided to ensure no mother would be around to ask for her baby."

The bile rising in her throat, Sara stared down at the photo of this man who now seemed even more of a stranger than he had before. "You think he killed them," she choked out, a statement, not a question.

"All of them would have given birth by now and none of them have turned up yet. If they just went somewhere to have their babies, there's no reason for them to still be gone." Halloran shook his head, his mouth curling as if he wanted to spit. "It's a good scam, I'll give him that much. He got a job around teenagers, especially teenagers in trouble—like pregnant girls—and took advantage of it. Talk about letting the fox guard the henhouse."

"Nobody knew about his family history beforehand?"

"Nope. When the police realized three of the girls were connected to the youth center, they started investigating. That's when they noticed several more missing girls, some they didn't know had also been there. The center's records showed they were pregnant, too. And these are just the ones we know about. There could be others, homeless girls with no one to report them missing, who he managed to take away before their condition was put on the record. Naturally, the police did background checks on everybody who worked there. That's when it came out."

"Did they arrest him?"

"No," he said, voice thick with disgust. "Not enough evidence. They couldn't prove any of the girls had gone with him. His bank account didn't show any evidence that he was getting rich selling babies—not that anybody with a brain would have expected it to. Any crook who knows his business would know how to hide the money. That didn't mean everybody didn't believe it. He was forced out of the youth center. They knew they couldn't keep him around."

"So where is he now?"

"Kendall? Dead."

In spite of everything he'd told her, that came as the biggest shock of all. Sara choked back a gasp, her eyes returning to the photograph on the table. She'd never expected to see the man again, but knowing for certain that there was no chance her child would ever meet his father still came as a blow. She squeezed a hand against her belly, suddenly overcome with sorrow.

"What happened?"

"He was killed just before Christmas last year. Hit-and-run. He was plowed down in the street like a dog." He shook his head. "Still better than the bastard deserved."

"You don't know that he was guilty," Sara said, a sudden hope surging within her. "The only thing indicating his involvement in the girls' disappearances is his family history, and that doesn't necessarily mean anything. You don't have any proof."

"Sure I do." He pointed at her, the motion accompanied with a flick of the wrist that looked disturbingly as if he was shooting her with a gun. "You're my proof."

"Me?"

Halloran leaned forward, his expression somehow even grimmer. "You spent the night with him. You got pregnant. And now they're coming for you."

A shiver ran through her. She'd gotten so caught up in his story that she'd nearly forgotten her role in all of this. "What are you talking about?"

"His access to pregnant girls had been cut off. He had to find another way to get babies."

The implication was so horrifying that she was speechless for a moment. "You think he got me pregnant on purpose?" she choked out.

"You are, aren't you? Took me a while to figure it out. The police might have decided they couldn't do anything, but I still could. I was watching him, waiting for him to slip up. I tagged his car and followed him that night to the bar. I watched you two go to that hotel, and I got your license plate number when you left in the morning." He shot a look from her to Jake and back again. "You two aren't the only ones who can run a plate. At first I just wanted to know who you were, if you were part of the scam with him. Then you turned up pregnant, and I knew what he'd done. For all I know, some of those girls from the center got pregnant by him, too."

"Why would he go to all that trouble?"

"Maybe it was ego. The same reason you hear about those fertility doctors on the news who get caught impregnating women with their own sperm. Or maybe he figured that as long as he was selling babies, he should get to have the fun of making them. What name did he give you when you met?"

"Just Mark."

"No last name?"

"No."

He nodded. "Smart. Using his real first

name makes it easier to avoid any slipups. Probably would have given you a fake last one if necessary, maybe an untraceable phone number to call that he only would have responded to if the message you left indicated you were pregnant."

Sara blinked, barely able to believe what she was hearing. "That seems awfully far-fetched. He would have had no way of knowing he would be able to get me pregnant, or whether I'd choose to carry the baby full-term. That's a lot of trouble to go to for a process that's hardly fail-safe."

"As for having the baby, you might not have had a choice in the matter. The girls must have been kept somewhere until they delivered, whether they liked it or not." Halloran pinned her with a pointed stare. "As for the other, I'm pretty sure he got something out of it either way...." He let the comment dangle.

Sara felt her face burn at the implication. "This is an incredible story, but again, you have no proof."

"If he wasn't selling babies and he didn't try to get you pregnant, then who's after you?"

"But you said Mark is dead," Sara said. "If so, why would someone else be coming after me?"

"This couldn't have been a one-man operation. As far as I can tell, he didn't have any medical training, which means someone else has to be involved to ensure the babies are born safely. Mark Kendall may be dead, but his business partners are still out there. Two of the pregnant girls who disappeared would have given birth after he was killed. I'd bet anything he kept records of the women he slept with to track down later. Hell, he would have had to. He must have left behind a list of possibilities for the others to follow up on in case something happened to him."

"I never told him my last name, either."

"Just because you didn't bother to find out his name doesn't mean he didn't bother to find out yours. You never went to the bathroom? Never left your purse unattended in the room with him?"

But of course she had, she thought with a sinking feeling in the pit of her stomach. They'd met at a bar, they'd both had at least a little to drink, they'd each used the bathroom at least once during the night.

"But why come after me so late? If these people are involved, wouldn't they have come for me earlier in my pregnancy?"

"I can only guess. Maybe if he'd lived and you'd told him about the pregnancy, you would have disappeared before you could ask questions about who he really was. Maybe they have somebody taking care of the girls who thinks he or she is doing a good thing, something they wouldn't be able to pull off if it was a grown woman being held prisoner. Or maybe they figured there wasn't much of a point. A teenage girl needs to be watched over to make sure she takes care of herself. A grown woman who made the choice to have her baby can be trusted to do it. Cheaper for them, too. None of the expenses and all of the profit."

"But in that case, wouldn't it be easier to just wait until after I give birth, then try to kidnap the baby? It doesn't seem worth the trouble of coming after me while I'm still pregnant."

"Better now than later. Stealing the baby after it's born leaves the original problem Marilyn Kendall faced—a mother to go to the authorities and let them know her baby's missing. Even if they go ahead and kill you, the police will know there's a baby they should be looking for. But if a pregnant woman vanishes without a trace, who's to say what happened to her, especially if there's no sign of foul play? And are they looking for a pregnant woman, or a woman with a baby?"

He shook his head. "He probably didn't even know just how perfect you were. A single woman, living alone, no close family. Nobody to raise a fuss if she disappears."

Not nobody, she thought. Eventually her agent or her publisher would, if they didn't hear from her for a while. But then, there was no way for him or anyone else to know that.

Jake moved closer, unforgotten though he hadn't said a word during the conversation, his presence a palpable thing. "She has me."

The words blindsided her. She peered up at him, wide-eyed, the breath knocked from her lungs. She'd never had anyone imply that sentiment before, let alone state it so baldly. For her entire life, she'd had no one. Now there was this man, someone she barely knew, offering something completely foreign.

She had him.

Disconcerted, she turned her attention back to Halloran. He glared up at Jake, seemingly far less impressed by the statement than she was. "Do you really think they'll hesitate to get rid of you if you're in the way?"

Terror ripped through her at the idea of anything happening to him because of her. She glanced at Jake.

He met Halloran's steady gaze, unflinching. "I can take care of myself."

"And her? You couldn't even catch me last night with that knee of yours. The way I hear it, the other one's being held together with a bunch of metal and pins, too."

Jake's mouth tightened, but he didn't deny it.

Suddenly angry, Sara turned her attention back to Halloran. "So what you're telling me is that you've been watching me for nine months?"

"Off and on. I quit the force to focus on the case when the official investigation wasn't getting anywhere. I want to know what happened to my daughter. I'm not kidding myself into thinking she's alive, but I have to think her baby, my grandchild, is out there somewhere."

"If you thought someone was coming after me, why didn't you warn me? Why lurk outside my house?"

For the first time since he'd started speaking, Halloran hesitated. His gaze slid away, a trace of guilt flickering across his face.

She had no trouble understanding the source of his reaction. He hadn't warned her because he didn't care about her. He only cared about catching whoever was responsible. She might have believed him, might have left town, and he needed her there, ripe for the taking.

She was nothing to him but bait.

As though recognizing what she was thinking, he leaned forward. "Now that you know, we can work together. If they went to all the trouble to come out here to get you, they're not going to leave empty-handed. You're going to need all the help you can get. I can protect you."

He was right about one thing. She could use all the help she could get. But not from him. Once again she was struck by that eerie intensity in his eyes, and she knew without a doubt she didn't want him anywhere near her. She didn't trust this man for a second. His goal was to find out what had happened to his daughter, not protect her. If push came to shove and more than one man came for her, she wouldn't put it past him to leave her to fend for herself against one or more of them as long as he got to capture one of his own.

"Thanks, but no thanks."

"Make no mistake, they're coming for you. I don't know how many, and I don't know how prepared they'll be, but you're going to need help getting through this."

"Maybe you're right. But I'm not interested in getting that help from you."

"You need to think real hard about this. Even if the police are willing to step up, they probably won't be able to offer much help. One gimpy jock isn't going to cut it."

"That 'gimpy jock' managed to get the better of you," she reminded him coldly, insulted on Jake's behalf. She raised her chin and stared him down. "Thank you for speaking with me, Mr. Halloran. I think we're done here."

He stared at her for a long moment, his eyes narrowing to slits, before leaning forward to gather his photographs. Returning them to the folder, he got to his feet. "Suit yourself. But I'm not going anywhere. I'll be around. I'm going to catch these bastards. And when I do, you're going to thank me."

Not likely.

He reached into his jacket and pulled out a business card, setting it on the table in front of her, perhaps recognizing she didn't want to accept anything from him.

"Phone number for one of the detectives on the case in Boston," he said when she didn't look at the card. "In case you don't believe anything I told you. He'll tell you about Kendall."

"That's enough." Jake took a step toward

the man. "I believe the lady said you're done."

"I heard her. I'm going."

Halloran strode toward the door, Jake following close behind.

The man stopped in the doorway and looked back at her. One last chill slid through her as she met his stare.

"Watch yourself, Ms. Carson. These are very bad people. Human life doesn't mean anything to them except to make a profit from it. And if they want your baby, they're not going to let a little thing like killing you and anyone around you get in the way."

Chapter Six

"It's all true."

Sara shut her laptop and closed her eyes. Her vision was starting to blur from staring intently at the screen for two hours straight. Not to mention she was beginning to feel sick to her stomach from what she'd been reading.

"What's true?" Jake asked, looking up from the other side of the table where he'd taken Halloran's seat on the workout bench.

She couldn't help feeling guilty that she'd taken the chair. He couldn't be comfortable sitting on that bench with no back support, his elbows resting on his knees, but he hadn't said a word of complaint or made any dissatisfied noises. Other than the occasional motion to stretch out his knee, he hadn't given any indication of discomfort.

"All of it. Everything Halloran said about

Mark Williams. Kendall. Whatever his name was. And his mother." She'd e-mailed Raven and asked her to dig more deeply into the details of Halloran's story than what she could find online. What she had found had been more than enough. She doubted she would be able to take learning anything more. "Marilyn Kendall *was* convicted of running an illegal adoption operation twenty-five years ago and did go to prison after murdering the birth mother of one of the babies she sold. She also had a son named Mark, who worked at the Great Start Youth Center as a counselor. Five girls with connections to the center did go missing, though most of the stories call Halloran's daughter Patricia instead of Tricia, which is probably why they didn't come up when I searched for information on Halloran and his daughter earlier. And Mark is dead. A hit-and-run late last December, just like Halloran said."

"Did you think he was lying?"

"No," she admitted. "But I was hoping."

"There could be more to it. I'm betting nothing you found said this Mark was guilty of what Halloran suspected him of. He said he wasn't arrested and Halloran couldn't prove it."

"You're right. But as he also said, then who is coming after me and why? This is obviously a coordinated operation. There were three of them, and they got in and out of my house almost without leaving any trace behind. It's scary, but everything Halloran said fits."

"You really think this Mark guy got you pregnant on purpose?"

She swallowed hard, hating the idea but unable to push it away entirely. "I don't know. I can't stop thinking about that night, turning every moment over in my head and wondering what it really meant."

"Halloran said you met this guy in a bar?"

"Yeah, and we went to a hotel around the corner from there."

"And you'd really never met him before?"

"No."

He frowned, something verging on skepticism in his expression, as if he didn't believe her.

"What's wrong?" she asked.

"Nothing." He shrugged. "I just wouldn't have figured you for the type to have a one-night stand."

Now, that definitely sounded judgmental. "What type is that?" she demanded, her hackles rising.

He eyed her. "Somebody who wouldn't turn red talking about it, for one thing."

She released an embarrassed laugh, keenly aware of the warmth in her face every time she even thought about that night. "You're right. It's not something I'd done before."

"I guess there's a first time for everything."

He gave no indication that he was going to offer any follow-up questions, which was fine by her. It really wasn't any of his business, or anyone else's for that matter. If they wanted to judge, it was their problem.

But the need to explain, to justify, rose within her, bringing words to the tip of her tongue she couldn't quite hold back. Because she'd spent almost nine months trying to explain it to herself.

"Actually, the only reason it happened at all was because I was trying to cut loose and put myself out there in a way I never had before. Not to the degree I ultimately did, but more than I had in the past."

She sighed. "The thing is, I used to be overweight." She shot a wry glance at her belly. "In a non-baby way. I never really dated much." Other than a few college relationships that had invariably meant more to her than the guy, she thought with a pang of regret. After a lonely childhood spent burying herself in books and junk food, she'd given her heart too easily, so hungry for a connection, she'd managed to convince herself that what they had shared was more meaningful than it was. Which had only led to her getting hurt more in the end than if she'd gone in with her eyes open.

"It was only a few years ago that I finally decided to do something about the way I looked. I started eating better, exercising, running almost every day—" She quickly swallowed the words she'd been about to say—*like you do*—not about to admit she'd watched him running out on the street through her front window, telling herself it had more to do with her own longing to be able to do the same again rather than the man himself. "Eventually I lost most of the weight."

Yet even once she'd become happier about her appearance, she'd put off making even a token attempt at dating, always finding excuses. She just needed to wait until she wasn't so busy. She just needed to wait until she was in a better place to start a relationship. She just needed to lose five more pounds, then she would try....

Except the five pounds never went away, she was never any less busy, and the right time never seemed to arrive. Until she realized she was almost thirty years old and she'd never been in a serious relationship, having let her fear of rejection hold her back for so long.

She swallowed, trying to push the flood of thoughts away. He didn't need to know any of that. There were enough embarrassing truths to share.

"Finally I figured it was time to make the most of my transformation. It happened the first Saturday in December. My agent was in town for a conference and we met for lunch. Afterward, I decided to stay in the city and go out instead of coming straight home. To force myself out of my comfort zone and see what happened." Not to mention the idea of spending another Saturday night alone had held little appeal, especially near the holidays.

"That evening I found a bar that looked halfway decent, so I decided to go." Because that's what you were supposed to do when you were twenty-nine—go to bars and flirt and meet people, not sit home alone hiding from the world. Or so she'd told herself numerous times that night to talk herself into it.

She'd taken a seat at the bar and ordered a drink, then sat there, unsure what to do next. For more than an hour, a few words to the bartender were the only ones she spoke. She'd nursed her drink and watched other people, trying to squelch the pang of envy whenever they had fallen into conversation with an ease she'd never mastered. Something else she'd missed during those awkward adolescent years when she'd lost herself in books and pastries, never going to parties and dances, not learning the social graces one was supposed to at that age.

She'd been giving serious consideration to leaving, ready to call her experiment a complete failure, when Mark had appeared.

"He sat down next to me and ordered a drink." She hadn't noticed him at first, so preoccupied with thoughts of leaving. Then she'd looked up into the mirror over the bar, and there he was.

She'd never forgotten the charge of that initial moment when their eyes had met and his gaze seemed to bore into her. He was gorgeous, so far out of her league that he was practically a different species, and she'd known she should look away rather than be caught staring.

After a long beat, the corners of that incredible mouth had slowly turned upward in a small, almost tentative smile. She'd nearly checked over her shoulder reflexively, certain he hadn't been—couldn't be—looking at her. She might have, too, if she hadn't been frozen in place. Then she'd managed to make her mouth move and return the smile.

"We talked a little, and it was nice."

"What'd you talk about?"

"Nothing really. The holidays. The weather. He said he lived just outside the city. I said I did, too. He'd come into town to do his Christmas shopping, but ultimately hadn't felt like it. He wasn't a big fan of the holidays, and neither was I. That sort of thing.

"We had a few drinks. After a while he asked if I wanted to get out of there." And she hadn't understood at first, thinking he'd maybe wanted to get some air, maybe was suggesting a walk.

Until she'd seen the heat in his eyes, and felt an answering warmth shudder through her, electrifying every cell in her body. And she'd understood exactly what he was asking. The yes had come out on its own, breathlessly, the idea of saying no never occurring to her.

"So we did. Neither of us lived close by. He asked if I wanted to get a room, and I said yes."

Hearing the words come out of her mouth,

she knew it probably sounded sleazy. Yet it hadn't seemed that way at the time. She'd stared into that face and those eyes and it had been pure fantasy. Where it happened didn't matter. All that mattered was that it did.

"I wasn't even looking for sex that night. But he seemed like a nice guy and the moment felt right. And I just—"

She paused, unsettled by the admission she'd been about to make. She desperately tried to come up with some way to say it that wouldn't be absolutely humiliating, only to finally concede there wasn't one.

I just wanted to believe that somebody who looked like that could want me.

No, it didn't get much more pathetic than that.

The mere act of thinking it made the heat rise in her cheeks. She lowered her head rather than let Jake see the emotion she knew must be written across her face.

"I just wasn't thinking," she finished lamely. "The next morning I woke up before he did. I…was embarrassed, and I didn't know what to say." And she was afraid. Afraid he'd wake up and look at her without the benefit of liquor or hormones or whatever had led him to fall into bed with her and she'd see regret in his eyes when he saw her in the cold light of day. "So I left while he was still asleep.

"A few weeks later I started feeling sick. I thought it was the flu, or something worse. When it didn't go away, I finally went to the doctor. I actually laughed when he suggested a pregnancy test. I think I was still laughing right up until the moment he told me it was positive." And nothing had seemed funny since.

"Did you use any protection that night?"

She ducked her head in chagrin. "I'm not sure about the first time. It was just really intense and happened so fast I wasn't paying attention. We did use a condom after that."

He hesitated a beat before asking, "You're sure he wore them?"

She opened her mouth to answer in the affirmative, only to have the words die on her tongue. Had he? She tried to think back eight and a half months, digging into the memories of that encounter, the intimate moments, the things she'd felt. That wasn't one of them. Because it had seemed too insignificant a detail for her mind to retain, or because it hadn't happened at all? "I—I think so. At least, I thought so." Oh, God. He had, hadn't he?

"Did you try to find him again?" Jake

asked quickly, as though more than ready to move past the subject.

"I went back to the bar to see if maybe he was a regular, even though it hadn't sounded like it. I spoke to the same bartender who served us, but he said he'd never seen Mark before. I even left my number in case he showed up again." She shook her head. "I'm sure the bartender just threw it away. I must have come across like a stalker, especially since I didn't want to explain the reason I was looking for a man whose last name I didn't know."

"What about the hotel? Who paid for the room?"

"He did. And yes, I did consider going back and seeing if they'd give me his name, or hiring a private investigator to do so. There was just one problem."

"What's that?"

She grimaced. "I couldn't remember the room number. Actually I'm not sure I ever knew it. I didn't go with him to the counter when he got the room, and on the way up in the elevator I was…distracted." Because he'd kissed her, so hungrily they almost hadn't made it to the room. And when she'd left she'd been in a hurry, ashamed that she was running away almost as soon as she'd stepped out the door, nervous he'd hear her leaving and try to come after her to see why she was fleeing. It seemed ridiculous in retrospect, but it had made sense in the heat of the moment. She remembered practically holding her breath until the second she'd set foot on the pavement outside the hotel.

"I'm sure a private investigator could have asked to go over the security tapes, see if there was some way to tell which floor we got off on and which room we went to. But even if the detective managed to convince the hotel to let him view the tapes, the idea of someone watching those private moments was too humiliating. I figured there wasn't much chance of finding him anyway, so I let it go.

"I probably should have tried harder, but I'd already decided to keep the baby and part of me was glad he wouldn't have the chance to reject it. I know what that's like."

"What do you mean?"

She laughed humorlessly and shook her head. "That's the ironic part. *I* was an accident, so you'd think I would know better. My parents got married because of me, because that's what you're *supposed* to do. For the sake of the child."

"You don't agree?"

"No. Sometimes, for the sake of the baby, you *shouldn't* get married. God knows, my parents had no business being together. They divorced when I was two and spent the next sixteen years fighting with each other because of me."

"At least they cared enough about you to fight over you."

"It wasn't really about me. I was just the conduit they used to take their hatred out on each other. They used to play this game where one of them was supposed to pick me up from school or some event, and whoever it was wouldn't show up, and they'd get into a big fight, each accusing the other of being the one who wasn't there when they said they would."

"You're kidding."

"I wish." She shrugged. "Needless to say, I learned early to always carry a book. I remember one time, after a typically vicious argument on the phone, my mother hung up and turned to me. She looked me straight in the eye and she said, 'You ruined my life.' And it's not like I could disagree with her. I still can't. If it wasn't for me, those two people who had no business being together never would have gotten married. They could have gone their separate ways and never spoken to each other again. Instead, they were stuck with each other for sixteen more years because of me."

"You're not to blame for their bad choices."

"No. I'm just the result." She cringed. "I promised myself I wouldn't make the same mistakes my parents did. I knew to always be careful. But the one time I wasn't…" She threw her hands up. "Here I am."

"Don't beat yourself up about it. Everybody does things they're not proud of. It's part of being human."

"I guess," she murmured, unconvinced, unable to think of anything but how stupid she'd been.

Mark's face, now fresh in her memory, rose in her mind, the way he'd looked that night. The image was enough to send a rush of warmth through her, the way he'd made her feel then. Except this time it was closely followed by a sharp stab of pain.

She pictured how she must have looked to him that night, perched on that stool at the bar. Alone, a little overweight, speaking to no one. Clearly nervous and out of her element. Someone who probably didn't have much experience and was less likely to have any unfortunate diseases. Who'd lap up the attention from someone like him with pitiful eagerness and agree to anything he might say. An easy mark. It seemed so obvious now.

She felt tears prick the back of her eyes, and she could only shake her head. "I should have known," she said hoarsely, unable to find the strength to raise her voice above a whisper.

"Known what?"

"About Mark. I should have known what he was up to."

"How could you?"

"You saw the photograph. Guys like that don't usually look at me. Of course he had an ulterior motive." A ragged sigh wheezed from her lungs.

The saddest part of the whole thing was that it had meant something to her. It was a one-night stand with a man she knew nothing about other than his first name. That was pretty much the definition of meaningless. But it had meant something to her. When she'd found out she was pregnant, she'd been so mad at herself. Besides the fact that she'd done what she always told herself she wouldn't, she'd done all that work and lost all the weight and thrown it away for one night. But at least she'd had the memory of that one night to hold on to. And now she didn't even have that.

Memories burned through her. At one

point her hand had fallen onto the mattress. Almost immediately he'd reached up and entwined his fingers with hers, clasping their hands together tightly. Somehow that single gesture had felt more intimate than anything else that was happening with the rest of their bodies. He'd pressed the softest, sweetest of kisses against the side of her neck. She'd closed her eyes as something cracked in her chest and she'd wanted to cry.

This is what I want, she'd thought, the memory of that single moment forever carved into her mind. *This closeness. Someone to kiss my neck. Someone to hold my hand.*

She'd managed to convince herself he had to be a good person simply on the basis of those fractured memories. A tender kiss. His fingers wrapped in hers. Because she'd needed him to be, and that was all she had to go on. Which was just pathetic. So he'd been a good lover, one who knew how to make his partner feel special, if he hadn't simply been going through the motions by rote. That didn't make him a good person.

Now that she knew the truth, those moments made it seem that much worse. Every ministration she'd thought tender now seemed so calculated. Every kindness felt unspeakably cruel. Every bit of it had been a lie.

And she was carrying his child.

Unable to hold back a shudder, Sara looked up to find Jake watching her. Mortified, she winced. "I'm sorry. I didn't mean to unload on you like that."

He was staring at her, brow furrowed, as though he didn't understand something, as if she had two heads. "You really don't know how pretty you are," he said softly, a statement more than a question.

"Don't." She turned her face away, against his words, against him. The line was so patently false that each word inflicted its own vicious pain. "Please. I wasn't fishing for an empty compliment."

"I wasn't giving one. I don't say things I don't mean."

The words were so blunt, so solemnly spoken, her attention was drawn back to his face.

No, he wouldn't, she realized as a strange thrill danced up her spine. Offering empty flattery would be like speaking a foreign language to this man. Even now, he seemed faintly embarrassed to have made such a personal comment, lowering his eyes and clearing his throat in discomfort. She still had no doubt he meant every word he'd spoken. And for a moment, she had absolutely no idea how to respond.

Then reality returned. A nervous laugh rose in her throat. "Seriously, Jake, that's nice of you to say, but we both know you weren't exactly beating down my door. And when you did, it had nothing to do with my looks."

"I didn't stay away because of the way you looked." His gaze slid to her stomach, then away again. "At least not the way you think."

Understanding, she mustered a smile. "It's okay. When I decided to keep the baby, I pretty much knew I was limiting my dating prospects, such as they were."

"Sorry. I don't have anything against kids. I just don't do family."

Almost in spite of herself, her smile deepened with amusement. "You don't 'do' it?"

He shrugged one shoulder. "What can I say? Some guys are cut out for that kind of thing, some guys aren't."

"You don't have any family?" she asked, suddenly reminded how little she knew about this man. Considering all they'd experienced in the past twenty-four hours, she was starting to have trouble remembering a time when he wasn't in her life.

"No," he said tersely.

"So how do you know you're not cut out for it?"

"I just do," he said, the words so short she felt him cutting off the thread of conversation as effectively as slamming a door in her face. "Besides, even without the baby, it's a bad idea to get involved with a neighbor. If it goes badly, you still have to live next to each other."

She nodded, unable to argue with his reasoning. They'd barely made eye contact before. She could only imagine how awkward things might have been if they'd had a relationship that hadn't worked out.

But it wasn't just her that he had avoided getting involved with, she realized. It was anybody. She didn't think she'd seen a single person visit the house since he moved in. Granted, she hadn't exactly been watching him all the time, but surely she would have seen someone.

It was none of her business. God knew she hadn't had any visitors, and she hardly wanted him or anyone else mulling that one over. No, better to mind her own business and hope everyone else did the same.

"Not to mention, when my knee gets

bettcr and I get back in the league, I'll be leaving anyway."

"That's right. I remember you telling the detective that. So your knee's getting better?"

His mouth tightened for a moment, unhappiness flashing across his face. "I'm seeing a doctor in the city. That's why I'm here, why I'm renting this place."

She hadn't realized he was only renting. It certainly made sense, though, with the sparseness of the furnishings and his plans to leave.

"You didn't want a hotel room or apartment in the city? I'm sure it would have been closer."

"Too cramped. I need more space to move around in. I didn't want to be cooped up in some little box. An old teammate who used to play up here still owns some rental properties in the area, including this place. He gave me a deal."

"This doctor must be pretty impressive to move here for."

"He's supposed to be the best. We're doing some intense PT and if that doesn't help, he's working on this experimental procedure that could have me as good as new."

She couldn't keep from frowning. "Experimental procedure? You mean like surgery?"

He nodded.

"Is that safe?"

"It's a chance. Better than the one I've got now."

"But there's also a chance something could go wrong, isn't there? You could end up worse off than you are now?"

His eyes narrowed on her face. "What are you getting at? Are you trying to talk me out of it?"

"No," she said, her tone sounding unconvincing even to her ears. "It's not my place. I guess I just didn't realize how badly you wanted to play again."

"More than anything."

"But even if you hadn't been injured, you couldn't play forever, right? You would have had to retire sometime."

"Yeah. Sometime. When I choose, on my terms." The fierceness of his tone, the tightening of his jaw left no doubt as to how much he meant it.

"Of course," she said, swallowing her misgivings. He was right. It was his life, his decision. She certainly had no right to voice an opinion on the matter. She was hardly in any position to question anyone else's judgment. "Anyway, I'm sure you'd rather be concentrating on your recovery and your surgery. I'm sorry I dragged you into my problems."

"I invited myself into your problems," Jake said. "Don't worry about that. You have enough to worry about. Speaking of which, what do you want to do now?"

That was the question of the hour, one she'd been trying to avoid thinking about. Sara sagged back in her seat, suddenly overwhelmed with weariness. She'd managed a brief nap that afternoon, but she was still exhausted, both from a general lack of rest and the mental overload she'd experienced that day which wasn't close to being over. Her mind was still going a million miles an hour, even if her body felt as if it could barely move.

"I don't know. I think I need some time to let it all sink in. It would help if I could finally get some sleep."

She wasn't going to kid herself that everything would make more sense in the morning. She had a feeling it would take more mornings than she had in a lifetime for this situation to begin to make sense. But at least with some rest she might feel more capable of beginning to face her problems head-on.

"Good idea." He pushed himself up from

the workout bench. "I'll let you get some rest."

He moved to the front door to make sure it was bolted, then to the kitchen to do the same for the back. She tracked his movements, drawn to the strength and solidity of his body, the sureness of every motion despite that slight hitch in his step.

Once he'd confirmed the back door was locked, he was about to step away when she called out, "Can you leave the light on?"

He frowned at her. "In the kitchen?"

"No, the outside one. It's just…dark out there."

She might have cringed at how absurd that sounded, except that his expression didn't change and he didn't comment. He simply nodded, reached over and flipped the switch next to the door. The outside light flared on.

"Thanks," she whispered.

"Sure," he said, finally moving away from the door and out of the kitchen. "Need anything else?"

"No."

He nodded tightly, not quite looking at her. "Good night, then."

It was on the tip of her tongue to thank him again. It seemed wrong not to with everything he'd done for her today—putting himself in danger for her, taking her more fully into his home. She also knew better than to try. He'd made his position clear. He wasn't planning on sticking around, didn't want her to get attached. So she wouldn't.

Even as part of her wondered whether keeping the resolution would be quite as easy as making it.

SARA JOLTED AWAKE with a start. Heart pounding, she sat there, leaning forward slightly in the chair, momentarily disoriented, wondering what had woken her.

She'd been dreaming. More like having a nightmare, reliving a memory from that night. She'd been on her back, staring up into Mark's face as he moved above her in the dark. There was just enough light that she could make out his features, but a shadow fell across his eyes, masking them from her. She could tell he was peering down at her, feel his eyes on her, but she couldn't see them, could read nothing of what he was thinking.

Except in the dream she had been able to see his eyes—eyes she'd thought soulful now revealed to be soulless. He'd been looking at her with contempt, with disgust, with cunning.

Waking up from that was a relief. Except

she didn't think it was the nightmare that had woken her.

A buzzing at the back of her mind grew louder, pushing away the last wisps of the dream, until she was certain of one thing.

Something was wrong.

She glanced around, scanning the room for the cause of the feeling. Something had woken her. She was more sure of that than ever. But what?

At least this time all the lights were on, allowing her to see—

No, she suddenly realized, her gaze falling on the back door. Not all of them.

The light outside the back door, the one Jake had specifically left on for her, was off.

Eyes wide, she stared at the window, peering into the darkness, terrified of what she might see.

Something shifted on the other side of the glass, barely visible in the dark. Something she knew without a doubt shouldn't be there.

The scream burst from her throat even before the thought fully formed.

"Jake!"

Seconds later she heard a thud from his bedroom, the sound of him leaping to his feet.

She scrambled for her gun. He'd given it

back to her and she'd set it on the table while she'd been working on her laptop. Damn it, why had she put it so far out of reach?

Behind her, the back door crashed inward, whoever was out there abandoning any attempt at subterfuge.

Twisting in her seat, she reached out, one hand clutching the obstructive mass of her belly, the other straining for the gun. She lost her balance and nearly fell headfirst out of the chair. She wobbled, steadied, then tried again.

Her fingers finally made contact. With one last little lunge, she grasped the weapon and started to swing around, her thumb working off the safety.

"Drop it."

The terse order came too late. She had the barrel up, aimed directly at the masked figure standing several feet inside the kitchen.

He was staring at her, his weapon also centered on its target.

Not her.

Jake.

He stood just off the entryway to the hall, frozen in midstep, his eyes locked on the man in the kitchen.

She froze, not sure what to do. Her first instinct was to pull the trigger, but what if he got off a shot, too? He could kill Jake.

Another man wearing a ski mask stepped into the door behind the first. He quickly took in the situation, then also centered his gun on Jake.

"I know what you're thinking," the first man said. "But let's be smart about this, Sara. Even if you shoot me before I shoot your friend here, I'm betting *my* friend is aiming at him, too. Between the two of us, I'm sure one of us can hit Armstrong, and you don't want—"

Before he could finish, Jake lunged for the man's torso, aiming low, under his line of fire. His attention off Jake, the man didn't even have time to react, cut off in midword. The tackle caused his body to fly backward, his arm to jerk upward. A muffled shot reached her ears. Plaster sprayed from the ceiling as the bullet hit home.

Sara didn't hesitate. She swung her aim to the second man, getting off a shot. He turned at the last second. The bullet whizzed past, landing in the wall behind him just to the left of his shoulder. It couldn't have missed him by more than a centimeter. Without looking at her, he dived back out the open doorway, disappearing into the darkness.

She jerked her attention to Jake and the other intruder. The two men grappled, a blur of motion that shifted and twisted every second. She aimed in the general direction of the men but eased her finger off the trigger, terrified. She couldn't get a clear shot, couldn't risk hitting Jake.

The two men exchanged blows, until the intruder finally lashed out with his leg. He knew exactly where to aim, delivering a kick directly to Jake's right knee. With a grunt of pain, Jake fell back, loosening his hold.

Freed, the other man rolled backward, toward the door. Sara retightened her trigger finger and aimed again, tracking his every motion. It was too late. Just as she was ready to take the shot, he, too, vanished out the door.

Inside she couldn't have been shaking harder. Outwardly she managed to keep her hands steady and her aim true as she climbed to her feet and slowly moved forward, the gun focused on the doorway, ready to shoot the instant anything moved in the blackness. "Jake? Are you okay?"

A muffled string of curses burst from his mouth. "If I ever see that bastard again, he's going down."

"Here," she said, holding out her free hand without taking her eyes off the door. "Let me help you."

"I'm fine," he growled, planting both hands on the floor and pushing himself up. "I can get up on my own, and the last thing you need is me pulling you over."

She rolled her eyes at the blatant show of masculine stubbornness even as she conceded he had a point. Even at her current weight, he had to be heavier than she was. And considering how unsteady her center of gravity was, chances were she would end up falling right over him, which certainly wouldn't do his leg any good.

She watched him maneuver his way upward, grimacing in pain any time he put the slightest weight on his bad leg. As soon as he made it to his feet, Jake took her by the arm, turning her and leading her toward the front door. "Come on," he grunted through clenched teeth. "Let's get out of here."

Sara glanced behind them, not wanting to turn her back on that frighteningly gaping doorway where God-knew-what lurked. "Do you think they'll come back?"

"Not back into the house. Not while you're awake and armed. But I wouldn't put it past them to try to take me out through a window just for kicks."

Her pulse pounded in her ears as she remembered how close he'd come to being shot, to being killed. He was right. He wasn't entirely out of harm's way. Not yet.

Releasing her briefly, he stopped to grab his keys. Sara grabbed her purse. An instant later, his hand was back on her arm.

Pulling the door open slightly, he peered outside for a long moment before throwing it open all the way. "Stay behind me," he said.

"I'm the one they *don't* want to shoot. Maybe you should stay behind me."

"I'm not going to hide behind you," he scoffed. His hand clamped on her wrist, he dragged her behind him.

Choking back a sigh at his foolishness, Sara kept her gun up and primed as she followed him. Her eyes tracked the empty street and searched the darkness for any signs of danger, ready to react if necessary. Most of the homes were quiet and still, the scene bizarrely peaceful. How was it possible that just across the street people were sleeping, safe and sound in their beds, while they were fighting for their lives?

When they reached the truck, Jake pulled the passenger door open for her and helped her inside. She twisted in her seat and watched him make his way around the back of the truck, too aware of the open target he made. If the intruders wanted to do something to him, this would be a perfect opportunity.

Her heart jumped when she saw a dark figure hurrying toward them from across the street. The light shifted as he moved, making it hard to see him clearly, but for a split second she was sure he clasped a gun in both hands in front of him. She opened her mouth to shout a warning, started to lift her gun—

Jake whirled at the last instant to face the newcomer, just as the man came far enough into the light from the front of Jake's house for her to see him.

Halloran.

Anger, hot and fierce, surged through her. So much for his claim that he'd be able to protect her, regardless of her refusal of the offer. She'd known better than to trust the man. How had he missed what was happening?

"What's going on?" Halloran demanded, wild-eyed, jerking his head from Jake to her to the house and back again.

Jake opened the door, his face tight with anger. For a moment Sara wasn't sure he was going to answer. "Somebody broke in the back—"

Halloran took off without hearing another word, darting toward the back of the house.

With a shake of his head and another muttered curse, Jake swung into the driver's seat and started the engine.

"Should we do something?" Sara asked. The question felt foolish even as it came out of her mouth. As predicted, once the opportunity arrived to catch the people he was after, he'd taken off entirely on his own. He deserved no more consideration from her than she evidently warranted from him.

"If he wants to get himself killed, that's his business. Mine is getting you away from here."

He slammed the truck into gear and sent them shooting out of the driveway. Once on the road, he spun the wheel and slammed on the accelerator, sending them tearing down the street and away from the house.

Sara kept her eyes on the passenger mirror, not sure what she was looking for but unable to look away. If Halloran managed to catch one of them, would there be a gunshot? The intruders' weapons had been equipped with silencers. If one of them shot him, there wouldn't be a sound.

They reached the corner, speeding around it. The house, still blazing with light, disappeared from view.

Jake released a breath. "Well, the good

news is, this time the police will probably believe us."

"Yeah," Sara murmured, unable to take any satisfaction from the knowledge that the cops might have to be a lot less condescending and far more apologetic this time.

Because while they might have won this round, the incident only showed that whoever was after her was growing more brazen. They'd come after her in a well-lit house, not a darkened one. Smashed through a door rather than sneaking in. Had threatened Jake's life. She had no doubt that even if she had agreed to go with them, they would have killed him.

And if they were willing to go that far already, it was terrifying to think just how far they might be willing to go in the end to get what they wanted.

Chapter Seven

"According to the officers at the scene, the light next to the back door was broken," Detective Tony Calderone said. "Maybe with the butt of one of their weapons or some other kind of blunt object. Probably right before going to work on picking the lock."

The noise of the light being broken must have been what had woken her. Sara shuddered at the thought of what might have happened if she hadn't. Would they have managed to break in, drug her and carry her off while Jake slept through the whole thing?

She glanced at Jake. He was frowning, clearly no happier with the idea than she was.

The officers had been sent to Jake's house while they answered questions at the station. Sara had had the feeling the first officer they'd spoken to was just humoring them at first, perhaps having heard about their earlier conversations with the police. When the call had come in about the damage at Jake's house, the man's attitude had changed considerably, and then Calderone had come and introduced himself.

Sara tried to pay attention to what Calderone was saying, even though they'd been there for hours and the exhaustion was deepening with every minute.

"We'll run the bullet from your ceiling through ballistics and see if anything pops up," the detective continued. "I have to tell you, I'm not holding out much hope. You said they were both wearing gloves and didn't touch anything anyway, so there's not much chance for fingerprints. We'll ask the neighbors on the next street over to see if anyone saw somebody parked at one of the vacant houses on that block. Realistically, though, if these were the same people who broke in to your house last night, then you can bet they went out of their way to leave behind as little trace of themselves as possible."

Sara suspected the same. She was just glad to hear the man concede that someone probably had broken in to her house last night.

"Any sign of Halloran?" Jake said. They'd

told him all about the man and the story he'd told them.

"No. And there's no car parked where you said his was. He must have returned to it and driven off before we got there."

And lived to stalk her another day. Sara almost wanted to believe that the man had succeeded at his mission, that he'd apprehended one of the intruders and dragged him off. But while the police had found footprints leading through the trees behind Jake's house, there'd been no blood or signs of a struggle, no indication the intruders had done anything but get away cleanly.

"I've got a call in to the Boston PD to find out more about this Mark Williams/Kendall and everything you told me, but it's the middle of the night. Nobody who worked the case is around."

"What about in the meantime?" Jake asked. "Can you offer her any kind of protection?"

"We're a small department. We don't have the budget for that. The best I can do is offer to have somebody drive by every hour to make sure everything's all right." At least he did sound sorry about it.

Jake shook his head. "Forget it. We're not staying there. If your officers are still there, we'll go back and pick up some things, but we'll find somewhere else to stay." He was still barefoot and didn't have his wallet, having been wearing only a T-shirt and shorts when they left the house.

"Thanks anyway," she said, meaning it.

The detective nodded. "Let me know where you end up and I'll be in touch, if we have any more questions or find anything at your house."

"Will do." Jake rose and automatically reached for her hand to help her up.

Minutes later they finally stepped outside the police station. Sara exhaled deeply. The experience had been better, but only marginally more satisfying. Being believed was a start, but hadn't gotten her far.

It was still night, but not by much. The impenetrable darkness was just beginning to fade, blackness melting into deep violet. It wouldn't be long before dawn began to creep over the horizon.

Jake opened the door of the truck for her and she climbed in. Once again she waited nervously for him to round the back and get in the driver's side. She didn't think her pursuers would be reckless enough to come after them outside a police station, but she wasn't about to relax anytime soon. She doubted she could if she wanted to.

Jake finally made it to his side and got in. He shoved his key into the ignition, but didn't turn it. He stared straight ahead out the windshield, his expression stony. After a moment he cleared his throat. "I was wrong," he said roughly.

"What do you mean?"

"I should have let you go to a hotel. You would have been safer there."

She frowned, her brow furrowing. He couldn't actually be blaming himself for this? "Maybe. I also would still be clueless. I wouldn't have talked to Halloran, and I wouldn't know about Mark."

"I guess that's true," he said, not really sounding mollified. "But it's time to do what we should have done in the first place. Let's find a hotel for the night. What's left of it anyway."

"Okay. Not around here, though. In the city."

He nodded shortly. "That might be a good idea."

"And it'll save us the trouble of driving into Boston in the morning."

He finally looked at her, frowning. "Why would you want to do that?"

"I'm not going to wait for the cops there to get back to Detective Calderone. I want to talk to them myself, to everyone who knew

Mark. I need to find out more about the whole mess from people other than Halloran."

He sent a skeptical glance down at her belly. "Is that a good idea? Don't you think you should take it easy?"

"As long as these people are after me, I won't be taking it easy anytime soon."

"I get that. I just meant that in your condition, aren't you supposed to be resting instead of running around?"

"I don't know what I'm *supposed* to do," she huffed. "I read fifty-seven books about what to do when you're pregnant, and none of them offered any advice for when you find yourself impregnated on purpose by a black-market baby dealer or you have people trying to kidnap you. I only know what I'm going to do—find some answers."

"You could always hire that investigator you mentioned. You don't have to do this yourself."

Sara barely heard him, the words nothing more than an aggravating buzz in her ears. For the love of God, why was he arguing with her? She gritted her teeth and clenched her fists at her sides, doing her best not to scream. "Look," she said tensely. "Pretty soon I'm going to have a baby, and before that happens I need to know the truth about how and why this happened. I need to know the truth about the man whose child this is. I need to know—" She stopped abruptly, words failing her, and sucked in a ragged breath. "I just need to know. Can you understand that? If not, you don't need to go. Just drop me at my house and I'll drive myself. I need to do this."

He surveyed her with serious eyes. "Okay," he said simply, calmly, as though she wasn't on the verge of hysteria. In her belly, the baby twisted, sensing her distress. "Let's go." He reached for the ignition key and started the engine.

His easy capitulation wasn't what she was expecting, and for a moment she was startled into silence. "Good," she said finally.

An unsteady sigh of relief choked out from her lungs in increments. She turned to look out the window, slightly embarrassed by her outburst, but not regretting it. Everything she'd said was true. She needed answers more than ever.

She might not like them once she had them, but more than anything she simply needed to know.

A HALF HOUR LATER, they left his house with a bag each and headed toward the city.

They rode in silence for more than ten

minutes, each monitoring their mirrors closely to make sure they weren't being followed, before Sara finally spoke again.

"So…is there someone I should be apologizing to for taking up so much of your time?"

Jake glanced at her in surprise. Her tone was light, but the strain was evident in it. He guessed she was trying to focus on something other than the questions that had to be driving her crazy. The hazy early morning sunlight fell over her face. She looked more exhausted than ever, her face pale and drawn. Her hands lay limply at her sides.

"What do you mean?"

"I just didn't know if I was stepping on somebody's toes by first staying with you, then making you drive me into the city."

"You didn't *make* me do anything. And if you want to ask a question, you should just ask it."

"I was just thinking that if you have the surgery you mentioned, you'll need somebody to take care of you."

"You offering?"

She opened her mouth, then closed it again with a frown. "Oh, you're right. I should have. After everything you've done for me—"

"I'm kidding you."

"Oh." She grimaced, the color in her cheeks deepening.

Jake smothered a grin. Hard to believe that the same person who came up with every foul-mouthed, no-holds- barred comment that came out of Brock Marshall's mouth would blush like that at a little teasing. "Of course. Not that I shouldn't have offered. I just don't think I'd do you much good, before or after the baby comes, considering I move about five inches an hour these days and a crying baby probably isn't conducive to a good recovery. I figured you must already have somebody to take care of you. You said you didn't have any family, so I thought a girlfriend or someone. That's why I thought I might be stepping on somebody's toes."

"No, no girlfriend. I'm used to taking care of myself. I'll probably hire a nurse to check in on me. That'll be good enough."

"No interested groupies wanting to play nursemaid?"

"No."

"So the stories you hear about athletes aren't true?"

"I don't know what stories you've heard. But I was just a guy in the trenches, not a superstar. Besides, I'm always careful about the women I spent time with."

"What kind of women were those?"

"Women I knew well enough to be sure they weren't looking for anything more serious than I was. I saw too many guys hook up with a woman they just met and wind up with a baby nine months later. I didn't want to get somebody pregnant." He winced and shot her a rueful look. "No offense."

Her mouth curved in a bemused smile. "None taken. Given the circumstances, it's kind of refreshing to hear. Besides, I didn't want to get pregnant." She shook her head. "When I found out, I was so mad at myself. I'd worked so hard to lose the weight and try to feel better about myself, and I'd thrown it all away for one night."

"So why'd you decide to keep it? Not that it's any of my business," he quickly added.

"It's okay. I figured this might be my only chance. I wasn't fooling myself into thinking my one out-of-character night meant I was ready to take the dating world by storm. I didn't know what the future might hold. I might never meet the right guy. The time might never be right. When I was actually ready to get pregnant, I might not be able to. But I did know I had this chance. I didn't want to look back when it was too late and know I'd let it pass me by when it was here."

"You weren't scared, thinking about doing it on your own?"

"Are you kidding? I still am. I don't know what I'm doing or if I'm cut out to be a mother. I've never really been around children, and God knows my parents didn't offer much of an example as to the right way to raise kids." As though just talking about them had revived her fears, she bit her lip.

"You'll be great."

She looked at him, a soft, surprised smile on her lips. The hopeful gleam in her eyes made his chest hurt. "Yeah? What makes you think so?"

"Because you want to be." Even before she'd revealed the number of baby books she'd read, he'd seen all the ones in her house. He'd be surprised if there was one out there that she didn't own. "It's the people who couldn't care less that aren't good at it."

"Your parents?"

He shook his head. "My parents died when I was a kid. I spent a long time in and out of foster care. I saw parents who wanted to be good at it and ones that didn't, ones who tried and ones who didn't bother. Most parents were exactly as good as they wanted to be."

"How many foster homes were you in?"

"More than I can remember. People might be willing to do anything for a baby, but I was six when my parents died and kids that age aren't in such high demand. Not to mention, I was a big, ugly kid."

"I don't believe that."

He shrugged. "I was always big for my age. And I admit, I was an angry kid. Didn't talk much. That made a lot of people uncomfortable. Some of the foster parents were intimidated. I never really fit in and didn't stick around anyplace long before being moved somewhere else. Another temporary home. Another temporary family. I've seen enough of them to know you're going to be great."

"Did you ever find a permanent home?" she asked, her voice heavy with a sympathy he didn't like hearing.

"When I was fourteen. My high school coach adopted me. Big Don Armstrong. He and his wife had a son, their only child, Don, Jr. He was a star athlete, maybe even better than his old man. Or at least he could have been. He was killed in a car accident when he was seventeen, right when he was in the middle of being recruited by every top college program in the country.

"Big Don was the kind of guy who wanted a son to carry his name and be the same kind of athlete he was. His wife couldn't have any more kids, and they were probably too old to start over from scratch with a new one anyway. He noticed me a few days into my freshman year. I was in a fight with this kid who was even bigger than me, and I was knocking him around. After the principal got through tearing us new ones, Don pulled me aside and said that if I wanted to take somebody's head off, I ought to do it in a way that I'd get something out of it. He brought me to a practice, I showed him what I could do, and he took me on his team. When it looked like I was going to be moved out of the latest foster home—and the school district—he took me in."

"And you finally had a family," she said with a soft smile.

He almost laughed. He hated to burst her bubble, but there was no point in lying about it. "No, I didn't. He was never my dad. He was my coach. Football was the only thing we ever talked about. And his wife wasn't my mother. She didn't want me around. Adopting me was all his idea. I never understood why she let him make such a huge decision like that all by himself, why she didn't leave him. I don't know that I ever will. Big Don died three years ago. The last time I saw his wife was at the funeral. She didn't have anything to say to me and I didn't have anything to say to her."

Her smile had melted into a sad frown. "I'm sorry."

"Me, too. We might not have had any use for each other, but she probably deserved better."

"I meant for you."

"Why? I got the good end of it. A home. A purpose. Something I was good at, something people wanted to see me do."

"What about love?"

"No great loss from where I'm sitting. I told you. I don't do family."

"Just football."

"Exactly."

"You must love it to want to get back to it so badly."

"It gave me everything. If it wasn't for football, God knows where I would have ended up. I wouldn't have been able to go to college, I wouldn't have had a career."

She hesitated a beat before asking, "But do you love it?"

"I just said so."

"No, you didn't. You said it gave you

everything, but not that you actually love playing the game."

The comment drew him up short. He wanted to dispute her words, only to realize she was right. It was a fair question, especially since he'd made it clear by now how much he wanted to get back in the game. Experimental surgery wasn't something to be considered lightly, even though it was obvious she thought that's what he had done. She didn't know just how much research he'd done to find the right doctor, or how he'd had to talk the guy into taking him on as a patient.

As he considered her question, a swell of emotions he couldn't begin to express out loud hit him hard. The truth was, he did love it, but not just the playing. There was more to football than the actual playing of the game. It was hanging around in the locker room and at practices, jawing with the other guys. It was about being part of something larger than himself, part of a team. And yeah, it was about game days, when the single-minded focus came over him and the adrenaline surged and he was in the zone, ready to take somebody's head off. The thrill had never gotten old, and there were times when he got lost in the moment and it was like when he was a kid, when he had brothers, and he'd been roughhousing with them and a man who'd seemed as big as a mountain.

His dad. A man whose face he couldn't even remember anymore.

But it was more than that. Earlier he'd told her he'd only intended to retire on his own terms, recognizing how foolish the words sounded even as he said them. Few had the ability to dictate the lengths of their careers. Injuries happened. Younger, faster guys came in to take jobs. Players who made too much were replaced by ones who could be gotten on the cheap. He was realistic enough to know how unreliable a career in the league could be, how everything could change in an instant.

Stubbornly, blindly, foolishly, he'd always thought it would be different for him.

Logically speaking, he knew he didn't have to play anymore. He'd lived cheaply, saved his money and invested well. He had a degree he'd never used. He had the luxury of time and money to figure out what he wanted to do with the rest of his life. Not to mention he was thirty-two, closer to the end of his career than the beginning, almost past his peak if he wasn't already.

But there was nothing logical about the

tightness that gripped his chest and the lump that rose in his throat, choking him, at the thought of walking away. They told him something else.

He did have to play.

It was what he was good at. It was what he did.

It was who he was.

And if he didn't have that…

"Jake?"

He jerked his head at the sound of her voice to find her watching him, a quizzical expression on her face. He suddenly realized he hadn't answered her question, lost in his own thoughts.

"Yeah," he said, his voice sounding strange to his ears. "I do love it. Hell, it's the only reason anybody ever wanted me around."

"I don't believe that."

"Really? I have four brothers, did I tell you that?"

She shook her head.

"I never saw them again after our parents died. Never heard a word. Then, two months after the NFL draft the year I made it into the league, I got a letter from my oldest brother wanting to meet me. What a big coincidence, huh? I sign a contract and my long-lost brother comes out of the woodwork."

"What did you do?"

"I had my lawyer send him a letter saying I wasn't interested."

She didn't say anything, her mouth falling open slightly.

"You think I made a mistake."

She gave a halfhearted shrug. "I can't judge. I know what it's like to be afraid people will disappoint you."

"I wasn't afraid," he scoffed.

"But you still expected the worst of him, right? I mean, it couldn't have hurt to meet him. Maybe you should have given him the chance, the opportunity to disappoint you before assuming he would. He could have surprised you. If not, then you could have walked away."

"No use wasting my time."

"Like I said, I can't judge. I would have at least met him, but then, I always wanted a brother or sister. More to share the heat from my parents than anything else. Maybe you made the right decision for you. I don't know."

"I do. And it was."

"Okay," she said simply. "I didn't mean to pry." Her expression revealing nothing but weariness, she turned her head and directed her attention out her window.

He bit back his irritation at her question and similarly focused on the road. She didn't know what she was talking about.

He knew who he was better than she did, had since he was fourteen and through all the eighteen years since.

He played football.

It was who he was, what people wanted him for.

And he'd be a hell of a lot better off when he was back on the field and away from this woman and her questions and her all-seeing eyes and the things she made him feel that he didn't begin to know how to deal with.

Chapter Eight

After checking in to a hotel and getting a few hours' sleep, Sara wasn't quite as good as new, but she did feel slightly more human. She wasted no time calling the detective whose number Halloran had given them.

Detective Mitchell Bates sounded less than thrilled to hear that Roger Halloran had sent them his way. He grudgingly agreed to meet with them, even if his expression wasn't any more welcoming when they arrived at the police station than his tone had been on the phone. His steady gaze scanned over her, lingering for a moment on her belly, one eyebrow rising.

"Thank you for agreeing to see us," Sara said as she and Jake sat, trying to make some attempt to win the man over.

A large man with piercing black eyes, Bates ignored the comment. "You said on the phone Roger Halloran gave you my name."

"Yes. He said you could tell us more about the missing girls like his daughter, the ones connected to the Great Start Youth Center."

"What's your interest in the case?"

She drew a breath. "Eight and a half months ago I…had an encounter with a man named Mark Williams. I believe you're familiar with the name?" He nodded. "The past two nights people have broken in to the places where I've been staying in an apparent attempt to abduct me. Halloran seems to think the same people who were involved in the girls' disappearances are now after my baby."

"In other words, people he thinks were Williams's accomplices."

"So he said."

He jutted his chin toward her belly. "So that's Williams's kid?"

"Yes."

"Huh," he grunted. "Interesting."

He didn't elaborate on exactly how it was interesting, simply staring at her abdomen in stony silence until her skin began to crawl.

"So what do you think?" Jake said impatiently. "Is it possible?"

"Anything's possible," Bates returned. "It does add an interesting twist to the case."

Increasingly irritated with his reticence, Sara persisted, "Is it true that Mark Williams was suspected of being involved in the disappearance of five pregnant girls who'd visited the youth center?"

"Everybody with a connection to the center was investigated."

"But he was the only one with a family history that would indicate a greater probability of involvement?"

"Yes," he allowed. "But the family background was also the only thing that made him more likely than anybody else. Otherwise, there was no evidence of his involvement. He wasn't seen with any of the victims in anything but normal situations at the center. His bank account certainly didn't indicate he was raking it in from some unknown source, like a baby-selling operation. Naturally if he knew what he was doing, he'd be smart enough to hide those funds. But there was nothing in his lifestyle to suggest he had an alternative source of income along those lines. His phone records didn't show any suspicious calls. There simply was no proof. We can't build a case against someone based on their family history." He snorted. "Hell, half the time we can't do it using their own history."

"Then why release it to the press?"

"You'll have to ask your friend Halloran

about that. He's the one who leaked it, sup-posedly to try to turn up the heat on Williams. It certainly didn't make him any friends around here."

Sara reeled at the news. She'd suspected Halloran was dangerously unhinged, but it was still surprising to learn he'd done such a thing. If Mark was innocent, then Halloran had exposed his deepest family secrets to the entire world for nothing.

Of course, she thought with an increas-ingly sinking feeling, that was only if Mark was innocent. "What about the fact that someone's after me now that I'm pregnant with his child? Wouldn't that seem to indicate he was involved?"

Bates eyed her shrewdly. "So you think his business partners are trying to capture you so they can sell your baby?"

"That's what Halloran suggested."

Bates seemed to consider that. "It would mean they changed their M.O."

"Maybe they had to, once the connection with the youth center was made."

"Well, it's far from the craziest theory Halloran's spun, I'll give him that."

"What do you mean?" Jake asked.

"After Halloran's daughter disappeared, he started calling just about every day, wanting to know if we were any closer to finding her, providing what he believed— most of the time, wrongly—was fresh information he'd discovered, spinning any number of conspiracy theories to explain what had happened to his daughter or the other girls. I probably gave him a little more time than I should have, but the guy was a cop—a pretty good one from what I hear before he quit to search for his daughter— and I felt bad for him. Call it a professional courtesy."

"But you don't believe him," Sara said.

"I didn't say that," Bates said carefully. "But I'm also not going to jump to conclusions because of some theory he's come up with. Maybe there *is* a connection between the case and what's happening to you now. Let me give your local PD a call and see what I can find out. I'll make up my own mind."

Sara swallowed a groan of frustration. If he was looking for proof of a connection, she doubted he would find it, given how careful the intruders had been. The only real connection she could prove was that she'd slept with Mark Williams. "There's a Detective Calderone who said he'd be calling you guys for information, as well. I would have given him your name and number, but I didn't have them with me at the time."

"I'll get in touch with him, then."

Jake frowned. "If you aren't taking Halloran seriously, then why did you agree to see us?"

The detective heaved a deep sigh. "Because I would love to get to the bottom of this and find out what happened to those girls and their babies. I keep hoping something will turn up. Hell, that maybe even Halloran might come up with something. That's why I'm not discounting what you're saying. I have to be careful before assuming anything. How'd you get hooked up with Halloran anyway?"

"Evidently he was following Mark Williams when I met him," Sara answered. "And when Halloran saw us spend the night together, he made a point to find out who I was. When I turned out to be pregnant, Halloran thought Mark did so deliberately and started watching me to see if they came after me."

"For almost nine months?"

"Off and on. That's what he said." Sara suppressed a shudder. The fact that the man had been monitoring her without her knowledge for so long had lost none of its creepiness.

"And instead of telling me, he decided to try to catch these guys on his own," Bates murmured. "Not that I could do anything. If somebody came after you outside the city, it's out of my jurisdiction. But I could have given the local police a heads-up." He paused, realization dawning on his face, then shook his head with disgust. "But they might have just gotten in the way of Halloran getting to the guys himself."

"That's what I figured," Sara noted.

Bates leaned back in his chair, that sour expression still on his face. "I actually haven't heard from Halloran for a couple of months now. I was hoping he was moving on with his life and staying out of trouble. I should have known better. I wouldn't have been able to, either, if I were in his shoes. Once a cop, always a cop." He gave them an unhappy look. "How much did he tell you about his daughter's disappearance?"

"Nothing really," Sara said. "Just that she was one of several girls connected to the center who disappeared."

"Tricia was his only child. His wife died when the girl was four, and he raised her himself. He was really strict with her, and by all accounts she was a good kid. When he found out she was pregnant, he hit the roof.

She wouldn't tell him who the father was, so he threw her out of the house and told her not to come back until she had a ring on her finger or was willing to give up the name so he could have a word with the guy. He says he regretted it almost immediately, and I believe him, but by then it was too late. He never saw her again. Not to mention it was his idea for her to go to the center after school in the first place. He thought it'd keep her out of trouble while he was working."

Guilt, Sara thought. That was part of the fevered emotion she'd seen burning in his eyes. Desperation fueled by guilt, the need to make something up to the daughter he thought he'd failed and lost forever.

As though reading her thoughts, Bates continued. "That's why you have to take what he says with a grain of salt. Halloran *has* to believe Mark Williams was involved, because it would mean there's a chance his grandkid is alive. Without Williams's background, there's no reason to believe anybody's selling babies, no evidence the girls are being kept alive until they give birth. Instead, somebody could be outright killing these girls, and their babies with them."

"But there's no evidence of that, either."

"No. I could spin dozens of theories of

my own for you and there wouldn't be a way to prove or disprove any of them. We don't even know that any kind of harm came to the girls. They all could have just taken off for parts unknown."

Sara gaped at him. "Pregnant girls who all visited the same youth center just happened to disappear and the cases might not be related?"

He gave a little shrug. "To be honest, the youth center isn't all that much of a connection. A couple of the girls were homeless and could reasonably be expected to leave town without a word. The rest of the girls were from the area. If they found out they were pregnant, it's not surprising they'd go to the youth center if they needed help or counseling. Different things could have happened to them and the center would still be a connection among them."

"You don't really believe that, do you?" Sara asked, her voice ringing with disbelief.

"Don't get me wrong. My gut tells me it *is* connected. But there's a big difference between what I think and what I can prove. There's a reason the disappearances remain unsolved eleven months after the last one, and almost nine months since Mark Williams's death." He gave her a sympathetic look. "Listen, as I said, let me look into your story and see what conclusions I draw about a connection to our case."

"Fine. You do that and get back to us." She reached into her bag for a pen and paper and jotted down her cell phone number, handing it to him.

"You're staying in the city?"

"Yes." She named their hotel.

"Okay." He rose to his feet, evidently calling the meeting to an end. "Then I'll be in touch."

Three minutes later, Sara and Jake stood outside the police station.

Jake looked at her. "Are you as tired of talking to the cops and feeling like you've gotten nowhere as I am?"

Sara chuckled softly. "It does seem to have been a recurring theme the past couple days, hasn't it?"

"More like a broken record."

"Now you see why I wanted to come into the city to get some answers for myself."

He grimaced and shot a glance from her face to her belly and back again. She half suspected he was going to argue again that she should be resting. Not that she needed him to tell her that. The ever-present exhaustion weighed on her and despite getting up just a couple hours earlier, she'd love a nap right about now. But the need to know burned too fiercely.

Instead he simply said, "So where to now?"

"The youth center. According to their Web site, the director is a woman named Kendra Rogan. I want to talk to her, to the people who work there, the ones who knew Mark personally. I want to know what they have to say about him."

He nodded once. "Okay. Let's do it."

THE GREAT START YOUTH CENTER WAS a two-story building that took up half a city block. With kids out of school for the summer, there were plenty of teenagers and older children flowing in and out of the building and hanging around in front early in the afternoon.

"Do you want me to drop you off?" Jake asked when it was clear they'd have to search for a parking space.

"No. I wouldn't mind stretching my legs."

He shot her a look, most likely recognizing the lie. She didn't want to be left alone. This was it, the scene of the crime, so to speak. The five pregnant girls may not have disappeared from here exactly, but it was still too close for comfort.

It might be foolish—there were plenty of people around and it wasn't likely her pursuers would come after her in broad daylight—but after last night she wasn't about to underestimate them.

Jake finally found a spot down the block and they made their way back to the building. Not for the first time, Sara noticed how Jake automatically measured his steps to match hers. He had such long legs he could probably make it there in a quarter of the time it took her. He didn't comment, didn't seem to sigh with annoyance or make a big show about it. He just did it.

She couldn't help glancing up at him, a sudden warmth flooding her system. He may not have wanted to get involved at the beginning, he may not have wanted her thanks, but he was a good man, better than she suspected he even knew.

He showed it again when he offered his arm to help her up the center's front steps. She took it without comment, leaning on his strength.

A teenage boy in baggy shorts and a basketball jersey was heading toward the door as they entered.

Sara flagged him down. "Excuse me. Can you tell us where we can find Kendra Rogan?"

"Down the hall," he said, jerking a thumb toward a corridor to the right before sliding past them.

They moved toward the hallway he'd indicated. Closed doors lined the walls. Voices came from one facing them at the very end. It was labeled Kendra Rogan.

Most of the other doors were similarly labeled. Had one once read Mark Williams?

The closer they came to Kendra Rogan's door, the clearer and louder the voices got. "I came here as a courtesy," a man said. "I warned you this day was coming and gave you ample opportunity to make other arrangements."

"That's not so easy to do," a woman answered.

"That's not my problem," he retorted. "The foundation has been a steady and substantial donor to the center for years and I'd think you could show some appreciation for that."

"Of course, you're right," a second man said, his voice calm and smooth. "And you have to know how much we hate to lose your support."

"Unfortunately, you have. I'm sorry things had to work out this way, but I've made my decision."

On the final words, the voice grew louder. He was moving toward the door. Suddenly aware of how long they'd been listening, Sara lifted her fisted hand to knock.

She didn't have to feign her surprise when the door opened abruptly. An elegantly groomed man in an immaculate suit stood on the other side. He took in her raised hand, hopefully making the assumption she'd been trying for, that she'd just approached and was about to knock.

"Excuse me," he said stiffly, his eyes clearly reading *Get out of my way.*

"Sure," she murmured. Dropping her hand, she moved to the side, allowing the man to slide past her. Behind her, she felt Jake do the same. The man strode down the hall without a word, the heels of his expensive shoes clacking on the linoleum.

"Can I help you?"

Sara looked up to find the woman and the remaining man in the office peering at her and Jake—the man curiously, the woman with thinly disguised impatience.

She scanned their faces for any trace of recognition, any sign that they knew who she was. She found none.

"I'm looking for Kendra Rogan," she said, even though she'd already figured out this must be her. After all, who else would be having a meeting in her office?

Kendra, a statuesque brunette in her early forties, met her gaze with a thin, forced smile. "You've found her. What can I do for you?"

"My name is Sara Carson. This is my friend Jake. I was hoping to talk to you about Mark Williams."

The woman's expression tightened. "Are you a reporter?" Kendra asked bluntly.

"No. I have a personal interest."

"What kind of personal interest?"

"Mark was a friend of mine," Sara said, reciting the lie she'd devised earlier. "We went to college together. I've been out of the country for the past couple years and lost touch. I just came back recently and couldn't believe what I'd heard about him and wanted to see if I could find out more about what the heck happened."

"You're Mark's *friend?*" Kendra echoed, her voice heavy with disbelief. "Mark's *pregnant* friend?"

Sara didn't even blink. "Yes."

Kendra exhaled sharply, the breath coming out almost like a snort. "There's irony for you."

"Can I talk to you about Mark?" Sara asked, trying to keep up a pleasant front.

Kendra threw her hands up and stepped

away from her desk. "I'm sorry, I don't have time for this. Not today."

"Kendra—" the man began, censure in his tone.

"Forget it, Noah," she shot back. "This is not the day to play nice. We're in this mess because of Mark and now everything's falling apart."

"An anonymous donor could always come forward as they have in the past to make up the shortfall," Noah said gently.

Kendra hung her head and gave it a slight shake. "If only I could count on that," she choked out. "But not this time. Excuse me."

Her head bent, the woman moved past them and out of the room, evidently disregarding the fact that she was abandoning her own office to them.

The man she'd called Noah watched her go, clear sadness in his eyes. He was a slim man dressed in a threadbare T-shirt and jeans that made him appear scarcely out of his teens. Sara's first guess would have been that he was one of the kids who made use of the center. It was only when she looked more closely at his face that she discerned he was probably in his early thirties.

"I'm sorry about that," he said, turning to face her and Jake. "I'm Noah, by the way. Noah Brooks. I also worked with Mark."

Sara recognized his name from the Web site. He was a counselor, as Mark had been. "Is everything okay?"

"You caught us at a bad moment. The man on his way out when you came in was one of our most reliable donors. At least until today."

"What happened?" Sara asked.

"He informed us the foundation he represents wouldn't be donating to the center any longer. Actually he told us as much months ago. We've just been trying not to believe it, thinking we could change his mind."

"And this is because of Mark?"

"The news about those missing girls being connected to the center wasn't the kind of publicity we needed. Even though it was never proven that the center was related to their disappearances, it made us look bad in the eyes of many people, which is exactly the kind of thing a big benefactor doesn't want to be connected to. I suppose he'll redirect his charitable donations to an organization with a less tainted history. I wish I could say he was the only one, too, but he's not."

"That's a shame."

"Yes, it is." Noah sighed. "It probably didn't help that Mark was the one who brought him in, convinced him to donate in the first place. Mark had a way of talking people into things. But then, you probably already know that."

Yes, she did, Sara thought wryly, even if there hadn't been much convincing required on her part in her own interaction with the man. "Sure."

"So you can see why he might feel particularly unwilling to support the center any longer. It must feel like he was personally betrayed."

"Can I ask you a little about the allegations against Mark?"

The youthful man leaned back against Kendra's desk and crossed his feet at the ankles, drawing Sara's attention to his tattered sneakers. "Sure, but there's not much I can tell you that wasn't already in the papers. And that's all they were, allegations. He was never charged."

"I know. I was just wondering if you saw anything, either at the time or in retrospect, given what you now know, that would make you think Mark was involved in the disappearance of the girls?"

"No, not that I can think of."

"He didn't spend an unusual amount of time counseling those girls?"

"Not really. Every staff member is available to the kids at all times, from Kendra on down. Obviously sometimes a close relationship develops between a teen and a staff member, and the teen will seek out that person in particular, but in general they can see whoever they want. I didn't notice anything out of the ordinary in his interaction with those girls or anyone else."

"Do you keep records of counseling sessions and when a counselor meets with someone?"

"Yes. Each staff member keeps their own records. The police requested copies, which I believe Kendra provided."

They must not have noticed anything atypical on Mark's, or Detective Bates likely would have mentioned it, rather than saying that his family history was the only thing that pointed toward Mark. Not that it necessarily meant anything. With each staff member keeping their own records, he could have purposely not noted when he met with those girls.

"Did you know about Mark's family history?" Sara asked.

"No. Did you?"

"No," she replied, because it seemed like the right answer. A man who changed his name to avoid being connected to his family history likely wouldn't run around talking about it, especially if he was in the process of re-creating it.

"That's what I figured. Mark always seemed like a great guy, but he never talked much about himself or his background. I guess in retrospect it feels like he was always holding back a part of himself. Maybe for good reason."

"So you think he was guilty?"

Noah fidgeted uncomfortably. "No one's gone missing since he left. What else are we supposed to think?"

"That whoever really was responsible knew better than to continue now that the authorities were poking around and decided to lie low for a while?" Sara suggested.

"Look, Ms. Carson," Noah said, sympathy etched across his features. "None of us are happy about the idea that Mark was involved in the disappearance of those girls or that he was abusing his position here. We're like a family around here, so believing it is like being betrayed by a loved one, especially given how much this place means to all of us. Every single person who works here has invested not just their time, but their hopes and all their energy into it. The idea that someone would take advantage of that is deeply upsetting."

"It's clear this place means a lot to you."

"It wasn't that long ago that I was just like these kids, needing a place like this, and I know what it's like not to have it. I didn't have the easiest time of it when I was their age. I was raised by a single mother, and my home life wasn't the best. I would have loved to have somebody to talk to and a place like this to come to back then. I love the fact that it exists, even if I'm beyond the age of taking advantage of its services myself."

"What about Mark? Did it mean a lot to him?"

"I thought so. But evidently it may have been in a far different way from the rest of us."

Sara's heart sank the longer she listened to the man. She could tell he didn't like speaking ill of Mark, but there was an almost hopeless resignation as he talked about him. He didn't want to admit it, but he'd had to concede Mark's guilt. And though he really hadn't said any more to confirm Mark's guilt than Bates had, the sadness in Noah's voice, coming from a mouth that had long since lost its smile, seemed incredibly damning.

"Do you know of anybody he was close to outside the center, somebody who might know more?"

"No, he pretty much kept to himself. I

didn't know about any outside friends he might have had."

He'd kept to himself. Like her, she thought with a pang. If he had been trying to outrun his past, it made sense that he might have been a loner. Had that been part of the connection they'd struck up that night, each sensing that they were both alone?

Or else he kept his friends outside the center separate because they were his associates in the baby-selling operation, a harsh voice whispered in the back of her mind, killing the ridiculous bit of hope the thought had inspired.

"Is it all right if we speak to some of the other staff members, maybe even some of the kids who knew Mark?" she asked Noah.

"You'd have to clear that with Kendra," he said with a trace of apology. "She's the boss."

Considering the state the woman had been in when she left the office, Sara doubted Kendra would be willing to grant that permission today. Not to mention there was a good chance they wouldn't see her again.

But as Sara and Jake made their way down the hallway back to the foyer after thanking Noah for his time, they heard a familiar voice coming from one of the now-open doors up along the corridor.

"I told you about this meeting twice. We could have used you today."

A male voice replied. "If coming all the way down here and seeing how much good this place does isn't enough to sway Tompkins, ganging up on him certainly wouldn't help."

"Well, we had to try something. Some of us aren't willing to give up."

"What's that supposed to mean?"

"You're looking awfully dressed up. Let me guess. Job interview?"

There was an uncomfortable beat of silence. When the man spoke again, his tone had softened. "I'm just facing reality."

Sara hesitated as she and Jake approached the doorway, not wanting to be caught eavesdropping on another of the woman's conversations. It wasn't likely she'd buy this time was coincidence. Given their mutual size and her lack of speed, there didn't seem to be any way she and Jake could sneak past gracefully, either.

"You might be willing to concede defeat, but I'm not."

Without warning, Kendra stepped out of the office, almost plowing right into them. She jerked to a stop at the last moment. She blinked at them each in turn, her shoulders slumping. "Oh, I'm sorry. About this—and earlier. It's been a lousy day."

"I understand," Sara said, meaning it. Now that she knew the back story, she couldn't help but feel sympathetic to the woman's distress. As with Noah, the center clearly meant a lot to this woman. Not that Sara was surprised. It was unlikely Kendra would be the director if she wasn't committed to the place. "Noah explained about some of the center's financial difficulties."

Kendra briefly closed her eyes. "I should have known Noah would probably talk your ear off, especially since he was particularly close to Mark. They were such good friends."

"I'm sorry if he shared something he wasn't supposed to. We didn't come here to delve into the center's money issues. We're really only interested in finding out about Mark."

The man behind Kendra snorted. "Ah, but the two are related, aren't they?"

Sara peered past Kendra to see the man. He was stocky and of average height, with wire-rimmed glasses and thick brown hair. Like Noah, he appeared to be in his thirties, although he was dressed more formally in a dress shirt and tie, a suit jacket tossed over the back of the chair beside him. Sara could see why Kendra had made the assumption he'd been at a job interview.

"Are you sure about that?" she asked.

Stepping forward, he glanced at her and Jake, pale eyes narrowed with suspicion. "Who are you? Reporters?"

"She's an old friend of Mark's," Kendra said. "She says she just heard about what happened and wanted to see what she could find out." Turning to Sara, she waved an arm at the man. "Allow me to introduce Adam Quinn, one of my colleagues, though perhaps not for long."

Adam sighed. "You know this may actually be a good thing. One less salary to pay means more money to direct elsewhere."

In a telling sign, Kendra actually appeared to pause and consider that.

"Are things really so dire?" Sara asked.

Folding her arms over her chest, Kendra eyed Sara closely. "You're really not reporters?"

"I promise."

Evidently deciding the hugely pregnant woman and the hulk of a man beside her didn't look like the press, her expression eased slightly. With a glance down the hall to make sure they weren't in danger of being overheard, Kendra lowered her voice. "I don't want to upset any of the kids, but I suppose it's hardly a secret. We're a non-profit organization. We require a great deal of money to stay afloat and don't produce any. We depend almost entirely on government subsidies, grants, private donations. Any or all of which could be imperiled by bad publicity."

"For which you blame Mark."

"Yes," Adam said, his face darkening with anger.

Sara could see Kendra forcing herself to strike a more temperate tone. "If he's the one responsible for those girls' disappearances, then yes."

"Is that why you fired him?"

"I didn't fire him," Kendra said carefully. "I informed him that I wasn't going to be able to let him have any direct contact with the kids here until both the police and our internal investigations were completed. I also may have suggested he consider resigning rather than let the bad press hurt the center."

"Even if doing so made him look guilty?"

Kendra's lips thinned angrily. "I have a responsibility to all the kids who depend on this place for somewhere to come and somebody to talk to. They are my priority, and no one person who works here is more important than them, not even me."

"Doesn't the fact that he resigned indicate that he really did care about this place and didn't want to hurt it?"

"That, or he realized his scheme had come to an end and he decided to cut his losses and move on," Adam interjected with a snort.

Sara glanced at him coolly. "You mean the way you are?"

She knew the comment had hit its target when his face darkened. His mouth thinning, he glared at her.

She turned her attention back to Kendra. "I heard the police investigated everybody connected to the center. Did you restrict direct contact for everyone on staff?"

"No," Kendra admitted. "But he was the only one with anything in particular pointing to their involvement. His family history was too much of a coincidence to ignore."

"Did you know about his mother before the girls disappeared?"

"No. He didn't say anything. Everybody employed here goes through a basic background check to see if they have a criminal record, that sort of thing, but his was clean.

I didn't think we needed to go back generations into people's family histories." She sighed. "My mistake, and my guilt to bear. If he was responsible, maybe those girls would still be here today if I'd just looked a little closer."

"Would you really not have hired him if you'd known about his mother beforehand?"

"No, I probably wouldn't have gone that far. But at least I might have known to be on the lookout for any signs that something was wrong. That may not be fair, but after everything that's happened…"

"At least you know for the future," Adam said, setting a hand on her shoulder. "And believe it or not, I do think this place has a future."

"You just don't want to be a part of it," Kendra said, shrugging off the hand.

"I just think it's time for me to move on. That might not be the case if not for Mark," he said with a pointed look at Sara. "But we have to deal with what life throws us."

"You sound pretty convinced he's guilty," Sara noted.

Adam pushed his glasses farther up the bridge of his nose, the gesture lending him a patronizing air. "No one else has gone missing, and the only thing that's changed is that he isn't here any longer. I'm not going to say I'm glad he's dead, but given the mess we've been left with, I am glad he's not here causing any more trouble."

It was the same argument Noah Brooks had used, but unlike the other man, Adam didn't sound at all unhappy to make it. "Do you have any proof beyond coincidental timing?"

"That and his background are far more proof than there is against anyone else, and that's good enough for me," he said, voice ringing with conviction. He shook his head. "I hate to say it, but it almost makes you wonder, doesn't it?"

"About what?"

Adam fluttered a hand. "The role of heredity in making us who we are. Nature versus nurture. Bad genes and all that. From what we now know, his mother went to prison when he was very young, so it's not like she had much influence on his life. And yet, first his mother, then him. It's almost as though it was just in his blood."

A cold chill swept over Sara, the sound of the man's words echoing in her mind.

It was just in his blood.

The same blood that ran though the veins of the child inside her.

The child of someone who might very well

have been a killer, the grandchild of someone who definitely was.

It was as though the man had ripped off the sloppily placed bandage Sara had placed over the wound festering in her heart, the fear that had been building at the back of her mind, fueling her need to know the truth. Now it was open and gaping and raw, flooding her head with so many questions and doubts she couldn't begin to process them.

Lost in thought, Sara barely registered Kendra excusing herself a few moments later, Adam murmuring something and turning away shortly afterward.

As if in a daze, Sara walked back to the exit with Jake. "You didn't want to ask her about talking to anybody else?" she heard him say as though from a great distance.

That's right, she thought numbly. She had wanted to ask that. "Not right now," she heard herself reply, as though the words were coming from someone else. "I just want to get out of here."

They'd barely stepped out of the building when Jake drew her up short with an urgent "Sara."

She lifted her gaze to him, then followed his attention to where it was directed across the street.

A familiar black sedan was parked slightly down the block, the driver's window rolled down.

Halloran had the audacity to offer a brief wave, acknowledging their attention.

Startled, she blinked up at Jake's stony countenance. They'd been so careful to make sure no one had followed them into the city that morning or when they'd left the hotel. "How'd he find us?"

"It could have been obvious this is where you'd want to come."

"Or maybe Bates called and told him we were coming to see him after I called. He could have followed us from the police station." Another, more disturbing idea occurred to her. "Or else he put some kind of tracking device on your truck, the same way he said he did to Mark."

Jake swore. She couldn't have agreed more with the sentiment. "At this point, the people after you don't even have to be following us. They could be following him. He'll lead them right to you."

"Which might be exactly what he wants. What should we do?"

"I guess that depends on who you want to talk to now."

She shook her head with a shrug. "I don't

know." She had too much filling her head. She could barely begin to process a single thought.

"Why don't we go back to the hotel and regroup?" he suggested gently. "We can relax a little, and it's probably the safest place, anyway."

"Great idea," she said, suddenly eager to get back there. It was a hot summer day, the sun shining down from high in a cloudless sky. Combined with her elevated body temperature these days, she should have been warm.

Except she wasn't. She felt the chill of Halloran's cold stare too intently, the effect only increased by the feeling that someone else might be watching her at that very minute, too.

As she and Jake made their way back to the truck, Sara cast a glance around them, studiously avoiding looking at Halloran, searching out every other space.

She didn't see anyone paying them the slightest bit of attention. It didn't matter. She could feel them. She didn't know whether the sensation was caused by something real or simply her raw nerves, but it felt as if there were eyes on her, staring intently. A hunter's eyes stalking prey, tracking her every move with cold intent.

She leaned closer to Jake, hating how exposed she felt, hating that she was probably letting her imagination get away from her.

Hating that there was no way of knowing whether it really was imagination, or whether her pursuers really were watching her at this very moment.

JAKE GLANCED AT SARA out of the corner of his eye. She hadn't said much since they'd left the youth center. He knew she had a lot to process, but didn't like how quiet she'd gotten. She wasn't even looking out the window. Instead she stared blindly at the dashboard in front of her, her head slightly bent, her hands clenched at her sides.

"You okay?"

"Fine," she said flatly. "Just trying to take it all in."

There was something disturbing about her stillness. He wondered what she was thinking and tried to come up with something to say to break through to her. Nothing came to mind.

He had to admit he'd admired her directness in her conversations with Detective Bates and the people at the youth center. No longer the shy woman with the retreating gaze, she'd asked her questions like a woman determined, straightforward and taking no prisoners. Maybe it was a long-buried side of her personality that she shared with Brock Marshall coming out, fired up by the life-and-death circumstances that matched anything her fictional hero had faced. Regardless of the cause, he liked seeing that spark in her eye.

Looking at her now, though, it was hard to believe it had ever been there. She just seemed spent, sagging back in her seat, staring at nothing.

Uneasy for reasons he couldn't put his finger on, he spotted the hotel up ahead. Thirty seconds later he pulled into the parking structure. Driving down one level, he looked for a spot as close to the elevator as possible so Sara wouldn't have as far to walk. The best available was one between an SUV and a convertible a quarter of the way down the row. He carefully eased the truck into the space, leaving enough room on her side for her to exit the vehicle easily.

Shutting off the engine, he unbuckled his seat belt, hearing Sara do the same after a beat. He was about to reach for the door handle when a sudden motion in his side mirror caught his eye.

He glanced over in time to see a masked figure, gun in hand, darting from the other side of the lane toward the window.

Pulse leaping, he immediately shoved his key back in the ignition and restarted the engine. "Put your seat belt back on!" he shouted, fumbling for the button on the panel to make sure the locks were still engaged. He heard the thump of them hitting home, the brief, low sound indicating they'd already been bolted, just as the figure appeared at his window.

The man reached for the handle, trying to open the door.

Sara screamed, the sound accompanied by frantic jiggling of the outer door handle on her side. Another man.

Jake didn't even look, already reaching for the gearshift to move into Reverse.

At the edge of his vision he saw the man on his side was already lifting his weapon, aiming for the window, for him.

If the shot came, it was too late. Jake shifted into Reverse and slammed on the gas, not bothering to look behind him. Almost simultaneously he threw an arm out to brace Sara before she was thrown forward. She gasped at the sudden lurch of the vehicle.

Jake yanked the wheel, spinning the truck at a ninety-degree angle, then stomped on the accelerator again. The truck lunged forward with a roar. He looked in the rearview mirror to see their attackers first start to follow, only to quickly slow as they realized there was no way they could catch up on foot.

The last he saw of them was one slightly raising and lowering his arm repeatedly, as if not sure whether or not to shoot.

Adrenaline still pumping through his veins, Jake sent the truck tearing up the ramp back to the exit, thinking quickly. "Is there anything up in the room you can't live without?"

"No. Just clothes."

He knew she had her laptop with her. She'd stashed it under the seat earlier in case she'd need it during the day. And he remembered from breakfast that she had her vitamins in her purse. "Good."

"Why?"

"We're not going back."

"What—"

Shoving his thumb on the window control button, he already had it rolled down by the time he reached the booth at the exit and screeched to a halt in front of the retractable arm.

The attendant leaned out of the booth with

an outraged expression. "Hey, pal, slow down! What's the hurry?"

Jake waved the magnetic room key that doubled as a pass to the garage in front of the scanner and thrust a thumb at Sara. "The baby's coming!"

The man's eyes widened. "Jeez! You want me to call an ambulance?"

"Be better if I take her myself."

As soon as the arm was raised all the way, he hit the gas and sent the truck careening out of the garage. He slowed just long enough to check oncoming traffic before turning onto the street.

"Don't you want to talk to the police?" Sara asked.

"Do you want to have another conversation where you say you don't who's after you and they say they can't do anything? I'd bet anything those guys are long gone by now and the cops aren't going to find anything. Even if they have to leave their vehicle behind, all they have to do is take the elevator up to the lobby and walk out the front door."

"The police could search their vehicle, figure out who they are."

"But which one? Do you know which was theirs?"

"No," she conceded, resigned.

"In the meantime, all they have to do is wait for us to leave again and follow. This is our chance to lose them."

"How'd they even catch up with us in the first place?"

"They didn't follow us back from the youth center. I was watching behind us the whole way, looking for Halloran mostly. They had to have already been here."

"Waiting for us," Sara murmured with slowly dawning horror.

"It probably was their best chance to get to you." It wasn't hard to figure out. Her pursuers' options were more limited now that they were in the city. They couldn't risk making their move in too public a setting, especially since they would have to transport her to their vehicle, in all likelihood unwillingly. An unmonitored parking garage, where all they had to do was wait for them to come back to ambush them, taking him out, drugging her and carrying her to their waiting vehicle, was as good as it got. Risky, but unsurprising considering what these people had shown they were willing to do to get to her.

"Do you think Halloran followed us here last night and they followed him?"

"It could be. Especially if he put a tracking device on the truck."

"Or they did themselves," she pointed out.

Jake swore. "We'll have to ditch it."

Sara nodded slightly. "And then try to find somewhere they won't find us," Sara said, a dejected note in her voice. Almost as though she didn't think there was such a place.

He wanted to offer some kind of reassurance. He couldn't.

Because he couldn't be sure there was, either.

Chapter Nine

"I'll be right back with your drinks," the waitress said, snapping up their menus from the table before bustling away.

Sara watched her go, then looked around the interior of the family-style chain restaurant. It was late afternoon, and most of the other patrons were senior citizens out for an early dinner. For the first time in hours she didn't feel the oppressive sensation of being watched, only because it was hard to imagine any of the people she saw could be the ones after her.

After leaving the hotel, Jake had driven until they found a rental car agency. Parking the truck in a garage several blocks away, they'd walked to the rental place, with Sara glancing over her shoulder every few steps, terrified that Halloran or anyone else would be able to track them to the garage and catch up while she was waddling down the street. Even after they picked up the rental car, they'd driven aimlessly for a while, keeping a close eye behind them for any pursuers.

Eventually, when she'd proclaimed her need for food, he'd pulled into the parking lot of this restaurant. They'd gotten a booth away from the windows, Jake taking the side facing the door to keep an eye on it.

Sara waited until after the waitress delivered their drinks to speak. "I've been thinking. What if there wasn't a tracking device on the truck? What if Halloran found us another way?"

"How?"

"He does have police contacts. He could be having someone monitor our credit cards, cell phones."

Brow furrowing, Jake appeared to consider that. "The same could go for the people trying to take you. We've been assuming they're following him. We don't know what kind of resources they have themselves."

No, she thought with a sinking feeling in the pit of her stomach. She hadn't given nearly enough thought to that. She'd underestimated them by assuming they could follow Halloran. They might have no need.

She knew nothing about these people, what they were capable of.

She swallowed a groan. "I can't believe after all this we're no closer to figuring out who these people are. It feels like I'm going about this investigation all wrong, like trying to bail out the ocean using a little plastic pail. It's just not working, but I have no idea what to do differently."

"If it were easy, the police or Halloran would have solved it a long time ago."

"I know." She sighed. "So where does that leave us? If we check in to another hotel, we might be safe enough if we stay in the room, but as soon as we leave it, they could track us again. If I could fly, I'd use my credit card to go somewhere out of their reach, but I can't. I'm not really up for a cross-country drive, but I'd do it if I had to. I don't think they'd follow me across the country." Except that she didn't know, did she? How much expense would outweigh the profit to be gained from selling a baby, if that was even their endgame? Could she even assume that? "Besides I don't want to leave until I get to the bottom of this."

"You really don't know anybody in the area who can give us a place to stay?"

"No," she said with a pang of regret,

wishing she'd made more of an effort to make friends, to talk to people, rather than keeping to herself. "You?"

"No. Maybe it's time to reconsider hiring some bodyguards. Even if you can't afford them, I can."

"For how long? Until the baby's old enough to no longer be profitable? We still don't know who's after me. I can't hide forever until these people give up. I don't understand why they're pursuing me so hard now, anyway. I must have made it clear by now I'm not going easily. As awful as it is to say, I have to believe they could find an easier baby to steal than this one."

"It could be they've already invested too much time in you. Could be a matter of pride."

"Or maybe they already have a buyer and don't have time to change course."

Shuddering, Sara cast another glance at the surrounding tables, the other diners having pleasant meals on what for them was likely a regular day. Meanwhile, she was discussing kidnapping and baby selling, which had become perfectly normal topics of conversation for her. How had her life turned into this?

"Even if we did go to a security firm, I

don't know one well enough to trust them, certainly not well enough to place my life in their hands. Do you?"

"No."

"And aren't most security firms staffed by former military and police?" The latter of whom Halloran might know. She knew she was probably overthinking things, granting the man resources that likely were unrealistic for him to have, yet how could she take the risk and not be? Halloran might not want to kill her, but as he'd demonstrated by releasing details of Mark Kendall's past to the papers that he would do whatever he wanted if it suited his needs.

Jake was silent for moment. "I might know somewhere we can go," he said finally. "My doctor mentioned something about having a cabin outside some small town north of the city, close to New Hampshire. Or maybe in New Hampshire. I wasn't really paying attention—he talks a lot—but it's supposed to be pretty secluded. Close enough to the city that we can come back to ask questions if you want, but far enough that anyone would be unlikely to track us there."

"Do you know where it is?"

"No, but I can ask. Make sure it's okay and maybe get the key."

"Won't Halloran figure it out? Since this doctor is the only reason you're in the area, wouldn't it make sense that he's who you'd contact if you needed somewhere to go?"

"Nobody knows I'm seeing him. I haven't told anyone, and I'm pretty sure his office isn't allowed to tell anyone without my permission. Halloran or whoever else might be able to figure it out, but it should buy us some time, at least for tonight. I don't want to put him in danger if somebody is able to make the connection. But the cabin might be our best bet."

She tried to think of any other flaws in the plan. Nothing immediately came to mind, and it wasn't as if they had many other options. If there was no easy way to connect them to the cabin, it might make a decent hiding place, for one night at the very least.

"Okay," she said as the waitress approached with their meal. "Sounds like a plan."

MAKING THEIR WAY to the cabin proved easier than expected. Jake had no trouble getting his doctor on the phone. The man had confirmed he held the identity of his patients in strictest confidence and neither he nor his office staff would breach that confidentiality. He also provided them with the location of the cabin and informed them where a key was hidden on the grounds, saving them the trouble of meeting him to exchange the key where they wouldn't be followed.

Less than an hour later they were on their way, both of them paying close attention to the cars behind them once again to make sure they weren't being followed.

According to the doctor, the cabin lay about an hour north of the city. It took them twice as long to reach it. After stopping for groceries, they took a circuitous route to confirm the lack of a tail. Then the turnoff to the road leading to the cabin was so tucked away in the trees lining the main road that they missed it at first and had to turn back.

Finally locating it, they headed down a dirt road surrounded by a dense cover of trees. The road opened onto a gravel driveway with the cabin at the end. Jake's doctor hadn't exaggerated about how secluded it was. From the front, all that was visible was the building and a short driveway. Both were perched just a few feet from the edge of a ravine, the sharp drop-off making it seem as though the cabin was sitting on the edge of the world.

Jake pulled up in front of the cabin and

shut off the engine. "Here we are. Safe and sound."

"Safe," Sara echoed softly, the word feeling strange on her tongue. She could barely remember what it felt like to be safe anymore.

Then she looked at Jake. His eyes remained serious, but the corners of his mouth quirked in a hint of a smile. The nervous flutter in her stomach slowly calmed, the tightness in her chest easing. She was wrong. He made her feel safe.

And she was. With him.

Don't get attached, she chastised herself. *He's not sticking around. He doesn't have room for anything in his life but football. He's made that abundantly clear.*

Even as the warning passed through her mind, she knew it was too late. She was already attached. Attached to his strength, to his solid presence at her side, to the kindnesses he seemed unhappy to offer but couldn't deny and the ones he did seemingly without even noticing.

But as he met her eyes and made no move to look away, she almost wondered if he wasn't getting a little attached to her, too.

He finally broke the contact, pushing his door open to exit the vehicle. She didn't miss the way he winced when he started to shift his legs out from beneath the steering column. A trace of guilt struck her as she realized the cause.

"Is your knee okay?"

"Fine," he said shortly. "Just a lot of driving today." He climbed out without looking back.

She turned her attention to the cabin, peering at it through her window before reaching for the door handle. It was a sturdy-looking, one-story building constructed of wood, a little fancier than she'd imagined, but probably to be expected given that it belonged to a doctor and not some rugged mountain man.

Safe, she told herself as she took in the isolation. *We're safe here.*

And she almost believed it.

Almost.

TWILIGHT FELL QUICKLY after their arrival. Sara had thought the nights were dark in their neighborhood. That was nothing compared to the impenetrable blackness that surrounded the cabin. Without streetlights or any other structures around, she could see absolutely nothing out the windows. The ones in the kitchen where they sat with the lights on reflected the room back in at them.

The ones in the dimly lit living room behind them showed only darkness.

On the plus side, it was so quiet around here they'd certainly notice if a vehicle approached that night. On the downside, anyone could still approach on foot, the darkness concealing a multitude of predators.

Sitting at the rough-hewn kitchen table, Sara kept her back to the living room and those empty windows. Instead, she focused on the reassuring glow of the screen of her laptop in front of her. Fortunately, the cabin was wired for Internet access, further confirmation that it wasn't the rustic place she'd anticipated on the way here.

"Raven sent me the additional information I requested on Mark and Marilyn Kendall."

"Anything interesting?" Jake asked from the other side of the table, cradling a coffee mug in his massive hands.

"After his mother was sent to prison, Mark was raised by distant relatives on his father's side. It looks like they're dead now. There doesn't appear to be any other family." She frowned as she scanned the document. "He had a bachelor's degree in psychology—the better to learn how to manipulate people, maybe? He also had a master's in social work. I guess those would be a perfect combination if the goal was to gain access to pregnant teens and influence them into going with him so he could sell their babies."

"You know, nobody we met today offered any concrete proof that Mark was involved in those girls' disappearances," he said reasonably.

"I know," she agreed. "But nobody he worked with did much to jump to his defense, either."

"If one of them is actually responsible, it could be they're trying to pass the buck."

"One of them, maybe. But that still doesn't explain all of them believing it, unless they're all involved and trying to make him look guilty."

"You never know. Or I could see them being so relieved that it's over and the guilty person found that they don't want to question it."

"I guess. I just can't buy that it's a coincidence that his family was involved in black-market adoptions and that pregnant girls connected to the place where he worked started to go missing. It would be too far-fetched for them not to be related. So if Mark was innocent, then what's the explanation, especially since no one seemed to know about his past?"

"I don't know."

"Then there's the little matter of these people being after me." She shook her head. "You know, there's that old saying about how the simplest explanation is usually the right one."

"Life isn't always simple, though, and there's definitely nothing simple about this situation."

"I can't argue with you on that." She scrolled down in the e-mail, then stopped, her blood running cold as she took in the words.

"What is it?" Jake asked when she didn't say anything.

She had to force the words out. "More details about Marilyn Kendall, specifics I didn't get from the stories I read. You know that girl she murdered? She didn't just kill her. She butchered her. Halloran wasn't kidding when he said Marilyn killed her in a rage. When her body was found, they discovered almost three dozen stab wounds on her. Her head was nearly severed from her body, which was dumped facedown in a shallow grave. A sixteen-year-old girl." She swallowed hard. "What kind of person would do that?"

"A pretty twisted one, I guess," he said gently.

"Yeah," she agreed softly, the word barely audible, her mind suddenly filled with thoughts and images she couldn't push away.

Bad genes, Adam Quinn's voice echoed in her mind, and the storm of fears swelled inside her.

The baby kicked, as he had for much of the day. The jab was hard and sharp, and she winced. A few days ago she might have appreciated the evidence of his vitality, the fact that he was moving and strong, might have pressed her hand to that spot on her abdomen and marveled at the miracle she'd thought this new life was.

Now she did her best to ignore the sensation as she closed her eyes and tried to fight the rising panic that surged into her throat.

Bad genes, that insidious voice whispered. *Maybe it was just in his blood.*

A LITTLE AFTER TWO IN THE morning, Jake got up to use the bathroom. Sara had insisted he take the bedroom, saying she'd prefer stretching out on the couch, where she could sit up with her legs extended. So he moved quietly as he stepped out into the main room, not wanting to wake her.

He'd taken only a couple steps when a muffled sound put him on edge. He froze, listening. A few seconds later he heard it again. Recognizing the noise only made him tense further.

A sniffle.

He turned in the direction of the sound. Sara was sitting at the end of the couch, her silhouette barely visible with only a single small light from the kitchen switched on. As he watched, her shoulders shuddered slightly.

He immediately moved toward her. "What's wrong?"

She jerked her head up. "Nothing." Her voice wavered, confirming his suspicions. She quickly lifted a hand and wiped it across her face.

"It doesn't look like nothing."

"Can't we chalk this up to pregnancy hormones and forget about it?"

He crossed the room and eased onto the couch beside her. "We could if that's what it is. I think we both know it's not."

She sighed heavily, the breath hitching as it left her throat. "I can't stop thinking about everything we found out. About Mark. About his mother." She released a soft snort. "And I thought *my* gene pool was a cesspool."

"The jury's still out on Mark."

"Maybe. We do know his mother was a

criminal and a murderer. If he did intention-
ally try to get me pregnant, then he didn't just
intend for me to produce a baby—he
intended to kill me. And if he was involved
in those girls' disappearances, it hardly
matters if he didn't actually kill them
himself. He as good as did. And that's the
blood that runs in this baby's veins."

"You don't know that for sure," Jake said
firmly, even as it became clear she was in no
mood to hear him.

She closed her eyes. "I know. You're right.
But I can't stop thinking, what if it is true?
And the more I think about it, the more convinced I am that it is." She gave her head a
tight shake. "When I decided to keep the
baby, I promised myself that I would be different than my parents. My child would
always know it was wanted and loved. I
meant it, too. God, you don't know how
much I meant it."

"I believe you."

"I used to think it was hard not knowing
anything about the father, not having
anything to tell the baby a few years down
the road when he starts asking questions. I
was wrong. It was so much easier when I
didn't know anything about him, when I
could pretend he was a good man simply

because I needed him to be. And for eight and a half months I thought I knew this baby. But now, with everything we've learned—" she drew a shuddery breath, tears shimmering in her eyes and shook her head "—now it's like my body's been invaded by this... thing, and I don't know what it is or what I'm going to do about it."

Grimacing again, she began to shift in her seat. She lifted her hand from her side and started to raise it to her stomach. At the last second she stopped, her fingers hovering just above her belly, before dropping it back to her side.

The single gesture hit him harder than anything she could have said. He pictured the room he'd seen in her house when he'd checked it for intruders that first night—the nursery full of toys, its walls covered with brightly colored paintings of clouds and animals and deep blue skies. He had no doubt she'd done that herself, painted her kid's room with the stuff a baby's sweet dreams were made of.

And now she couldn't even bring herself to touch her stomach.

"This kid is still yours," he said, his voice damn near as rough as hers.

"Is it? I'm not the one who planned it. I'm

not the one who went to so much trouble to ensure it would come into being. I'm not the one who wanted it that badly. For me, it was just an accident, not a plan come to fruition."

"It doesn't matter. It's still half yours."

"I'm not sure that says much, not to mention it's the other half that really worries me."

"Even if he was a bad guy, that doesn't mean your kid will be. Are you like your parents?"

She spread her hands, a laugh tinged with hysteria bursting from her lips. "I didn't want to think so, but here I am."

"The difference is your kid will have you," he said fiercely. "That's more important than how it happened. As long as this kid has you, it'll be okay."

She raised watery eyes to meet his. A desperate hope shimmered through the tears. "You think so?"

"I do," he said solemnly, imbuing the word with every ounce of conviction he could.

For a long moment she just stared up at him. A reluctant smile pulled at one corner of her mouth. "I thought you weren't good at this family stuff."

He looked away, embarrassed. "Just saying what makes sense."

"Or some things just come naturally to some people."

"I don't know about that."

"I do," she said, her voice ringing with certainty.

The feeling of her fingers on his cheek sent a jolt straight through his system. He turned into the touch, meeting her eyes again.

"It makes me sad that you think football is all you have to offer," she said.

He had to swallow hard to clear the lump that suddenly formed in his throat. "It makes me sad that you don't know how great you are."

Her eyes skittered away, as he knew they would, her discomfort clear.

A few moments later she raised them again.

"I wish I'd waited," she whispered. "I wish I'd met you first."

Almost as soon as the words left her mouth, he saw a hint of sadness cloud her gaze and he knew what she was thinking. If it wasn't for the baby and everything that surrounded it, they never would have met in the first place. Neither of them would have made any attempt to get to know the other person. They'd be back to exchanging polite nods across the distance. The thought made him sadder than anything he could imagine.

"Maybe things happen for a reason," he said.

A soft smile curved her lips. "Maybe they do."

She'd leaned closer when she'd touched his face, and without realizing it, he'd done the same in response to that touch. Their faces were now mere inches apart. Her hand was still on his cheek, her fingers easily the softest thing he'd felt in a long time. He felt a rolling heat shudder through his body starting from where her skin made contact with his.

She really was pretty, he thought, especially up close. Even the round fullness of her face couldn't disguise the attractiveness of her features. When she smiled her whole face lit up. It was a face made for smiling. The knowledge that she did it so seldom seemed wrong. Her eyes were dark brown, a shade he'd never really thought of as especially beautiful. It was on her.

Her lips were full and looked incredibly soft. He felt a hard tug inside, the instinctive response to her closeness telling him what to do now. What he wanted. What he needed. It was the same instinct he'd tried denying as hard as he could for a while now. Probably should. But damned if he could remember why.

He leaned forward and pressed his lips to

hers. She didn't react at first, not resisting, but not responding either. Then, slowly, tentatively, she began to counter his movements with her own. Her lips worked against his, first hesitantly, then with growing eagerness. He immediately recognized her inexperience, her motions slightly awkward. She hadn't been kissed much, or at the very least, she hadn't been kissed right.

But what she lacked in finesse she made up for in enthusiasm. Their mouths met, parted, and rejoined, faster, then harder. He pushed his tongue over her lower lip and into her mouth. It took her a few seconds to respond, her tongue darting out, sliding against his.

He reached out and cupped the back of her head in the palm of his right hand, even as she threaded her fingers through his hair, drawing him closer.

He kissed her with hunger. With need. But there was something else, too, something more, something he'd never felt before, something that struck a nervous pang in his chest even as he deepened the kiss, wanting more, unable to get enough. Even as he wondered if he ever could.

Almost simultaneously they broke the kiss, their breaths coming in quick, sharp pants. But they didn't move apart entirely. He rested his forehead against hers and closed his eyes, breathing in the scent of her, feeling the erratic throb of her pulse beneath his thumb.

He opened his eyes again as she tilted her head up to look at him.

"However it happened, I'm glad I met you," she whispered.

His heart squeezed in his chest, reminding him of everything he knew. He was all wrong for this woman. He wasn't what she needed, and he couldn't be.

He couldn't tell her that. Not now. Not with his pulse racing and the blood pounding through every inch of his body. Not with her looking at him like that, her expression open and expectant, her mouth still moist from his tongue.

Not when he increasingly wanted to deny it himself, wanted to try being that man, no matter how impossible he knew it to be.

But there was one truth he could offer her.

"Me, too," he said, his voice sounding strangely rough to his ears.

Her smile deepened, the look on her face so sweetly vulnerable that the thought of anyone hurting this woman—him included—filled him with a sudden fierce rage.

It wasn't going to happen. He promised himself he wouldn't let it.

Even as that voice deep inside whispered that he might hurt her most of all.

Chapter Ten

Jake leaned back against the kitchen counter and watched Sara work at her laptop in the morning sunlight, her steady gaze focused on the monitor, her soft lips pursed in concentration.

Neither of them had said anything about last night. Neither of them had to. It was there, hanging in the air between them, the space charged with something that hadn't been there before. Energy. Electricity. Awareness. He didn't know what it was, any more than he knew what to do about it. All he knew was he couldn't stop watching her, his eyes tracking her every move. Even when he realized he was doing it and made a conscious effort to stop, he'd find himself doing it again a short while later.

As he watched, the tip of her tongue slid out of her mouth to moisten her lips. He caught the flicker of her eyes as they darted in his direction and away again. She seemed nervous. Hell, he understood the feeling, as the uneasy rumble in his belly proved too well.

Turning away, he dumped the full cup of coffee he was holding into the sink and started to rinse the cup. Something had changed between them, but so many things hadn't, enough to render last night moot.

He cleared his throat, needing a distraction for them both. "What are you looking at?"

"Raven sent me information on some of the employees from the youth center," she murmured.

He turned back to face her. "Already? Doesn't she ever sleep?"

"I'm sure she'd say no."

"Is this Raven an actual person or some kind of fancy computer program that spits out answers to any question you ask?"

Her lips curved indulgently. "She's an actual person. I've actually spoken to her on the phone."

"You do know they have those computer programs that simulate human voices, right?" he teased.

After a beat, she laughed, her whole face lighting up with it, transformed by it. "Yes, trust me, she's a real person."

God, he loved her smile.

Damned if he knew what to do about it.

"So which employees?" he asked roughly.

"Kendra Rogan, Adam Quinn and Noah Brooks, since those were the three names I had, along with a few others she was able to dig up on her own. It's like Halloran and Bates both said. On the surface, none of these people appear to be flush with large amounts of cash any more than Mark did. For instance, when it comes to housing, they all rent instead of own. They each own older model cars, nothing fancy. And we saw for ourselves that Noah doesn't even look like he can afford new shoes. I can understand someone not wanting to make it look like they have much money if they're doing something illegal to earn it, but I think he could get away with buying at least one decent pair of shoes without seeming suspicious. There may be employees with questionable spending habits, but if so, none of them are on this list."

"Does it have to be an employee? These people could be using another teenager to lure the girls away, maybe someone to claim he or she knows someone who can help. That person may not even necessarily know they're doing anything wrong. They could legitimately think they're helping."

She tilted her head and appeared to think about it. "I don't see how they could not know it's wrong when the girls disappear and are never heard from again, but I could definitely buy another teenager being involved. Unfortunately, if that's the case, I wouldn't know where to begin tracking him or her down. I really don't think Kendra will let me talk to the teenagers at the center."

"So where does that leave us?"

"Nowhere, I guess. At this point the best way to figure out who's after me and whether they're connected to Mark would probably be to wait for them to show up and ask them, and that seems way too dangerous." With a sigh, she pushed her chair back from the table. "In the meantime, I have to use the bathroom." She rolled her eyes. "Again."

He stepped forward and offered his hands to help her from her seat. A grateful smile touched her lips, only to turn into a pained wince when she was halfway out of the chair.

"Are you okay?"

Letting out a slow deep breath, she rubbed a hand along the underside of her belly. "Just a little twinge. I think it's indigestion. Must be something I ate. Not to mention my back is killing me. I've been sitting too long." Waving a hand, she padded to the bathroom.

He watched her go, unable to keep the frown from his face.

She'd barely closed the door when the sound of tires crunching on dirt put him on alert. He quickly moved to the front window.

A familiar black sedan came to a stop behind the rental car.

"Damn it." Grabbing Sara's gun, he reached for the door. He stepped outside just as Halloran climbed out of his car, hoping to get rid of the man before he could upset Sara. "What the hell are you doing here? How'd you find us?"

Unfazed by Jake's anger, Halloran slowly turned in a circle, checking out the property. "I've been keeping an eye on her for almost nine months. You didn't think I'd check out the guy who moved in next door to her, late in her pregnancy? I found out about that doctor you're seeing."

Jake swore.

"You don't know many people around here. Made sense you'd ask him for help." He stopped, turning to face Jake. "This isn't a good location. It's too isolated. If they arrive, there's no way you'll be able to get out of here."

Furious, Jake stalked toward the man. "If they arrive, it's because you led them here."

Halloran stared back, unrepentant. "Where

she goes, I go. And if I could find this place, anybody else could, too. You need to go back to your house. Or hers. Plenty of available exits there."

"Not to mention easier for you to keep an eye on us."

"Would that be such a bad thing? You could use the backup."

"Except you wouldn't be there to back us up. You're only interested in catching the men who are after Sara."

"What's the difference? If they come after her, you can't take them all on yourself."

"I've done all right so far. And I wouldn't put it past you to leave her to fend for herself as long as you can catch one of them."

"These guys need to be stopped."

"Starting with Sara, not after—"

The roar of an engine cut off his words. Whipping his head toward the sound, Jake didn't even have time to react before a van burst out of the trees and lurched into the driveway. The windows were open, allowing him to see the two men in the front seat, both tugging ski masks down over their faces.

It was exactly as he'd said. Halloran had led Sara's pursuers right to her.

Jake saw the gun emerge from the passenger window seconds before the gunman started firing.

He reacted on instinct, diving out of its sights with no thought to his direction. Gunfire filled his ears. He tensed in midair, ready to follow his momentum and keep rolling as soon as he hit the ground.

Except he didn't.

He realized what was going to happen seconds before it did. Remembered just how close he'd been to the edge of the ravine. Knew he'd dived right over it.

Then he was in a free fall, tumbling over and over down into the gully. Instead of the ground, he first made impact with a jutting branch, then another. They slapped at him, one after another, whipping at his face and arms and legs. Then, finally, he hit earth, crashing against it hard enough that it felt as if he'd fallen ten stories. A jolt shot through his leg, jarring his bad knee. He almost let out a yelp of pain. He swallowed it as he kept rolling.

At last he felt his momentum slow. He rolled one final time, flopping over onto his back, and stopped. Only then did he realize he still had Sara's gun clutched in his hand, somehow holding on to it through the fall. He lay utterly still, sensing them watching from above. The thick undergrowth was all he saw, the greenery covering his face. He could only hope it covered the rest of him.

Moments later he heard more shots and the dull thud of something hitting the ground in quick succession a few yards away.

They were spraying the leaves with bullets.

He sucked in a breath through his teeth at the ache in his knee and readied himself for a greater pain, the impact of bullets into flesh.

Then nothing.

Silence filled the air. His heart thundering in his ears, his knee throbbing, he tried not to move a muscle and kept his breathing as shallow and silent as possible.

He slowly counted to a hundred, even as every instinct screamed for him to get back on his feet. Sara was alone, defenseless. He had to get to her.

But he couldn't. Not yet. He couldn't betray his location or his survival of the fall as long as someone was up there to hear. Then there would be nothing he could do for her.

So he waited and counted, forcing himself to take a deep breath between each number to keep from rushing through them.

When he finally hit one hundred, he waited a heartbeat longer, listening for voices or footsteps up above, trying to sense anyone watching.

Neither hearing nor sensing anyone, he slowly raised his head and pushed his face above the leaves just enough to see. Body tensed in readiness, he prepared himself to react to whatever he might find.

No one peered down at him from above. The top of the ravine remained empty.

He quickly climbed to his feet, shoving the gun into the back of his waistband and doing his best to remain as quiet as possible. As soon as he put weight on it, pain shot through his bad leg. Sucking in a breath, he leaned on his good leg and tilted his head back to survey the ravine's height.

No matter how long his fall had seemed to last, the ravine wasn't that high, maybe a couple dozen feet. He could make it out. He had to.

Gripping a few branches just above his head, he tested their strength. They should hold.

He planted his good leg, took a deep breath, then tried his aching bad one. The knee threatened to buckle, the whole thing feeling like it was about to rip apart again.

Gritting his teeth, he ignored it, forcing a single thought to the forefront of his mind—Sara—and started to climb.

SARA HAD JUST STEPPED out of the bathroom, still rubbing her belly against the dull ache that had settled there, when she heard the first gunshot.

Then it was all she heard, a rapid succession of shots that all mixed together, echoes and fresh shots combined, which made it sound as if they were going on forever.

She froze, the twinge in her abdomen forgotten. Someone was out there. More than one someone from the sound of the shots.

And they wouldn't be firing if there was no one to shoot at.

No.

She swung her head, frantically searching for some sign of Jake, already knowing what she'd find.

Nothing. The room's emptiness mocked her.

Her gaze went to the spot where she'd left her gun the night before—the coffee table in front of the couch. It wasn't there. He must have taken it.

Except she was familiar enough with the sound of her own weapon firing that she knew it hadn't been responsible for all those shots, if it had contributed at all.

She felt tears begin to burn the back of her eyes. She ignored the sensation, couldn't spare the time even as fear began to squeeze her heart, a searing pain in her chest. Whatever was happening out there, whatever had happened to Jake, there was nothing she could do. Because if someone had gotten to him, they would be coming after her next.

She hurried to the door as fast as she could, every step seeming impossibly slow, and reached for the lock. Her fingers gripping the dead bolt, she hesitated.

If Jake was out there, if he was able to retreat to the house, she'd be locking him out.

A tear slipped free, stinging as it slid down her cheek.

They'd stopped firing. If Jake could have come back, he would have by now.

She heard doors slamming, then footsteps pounding closer.

She slammed the bolt home and whirled around, now seeking something else. A weapon.

Lurching across the room, Sara grabbed the only thing within reach—a table lamp with a heavy base—ripping off the shade and wielding it by the neck. She spun back around just as the footsteps reached the threshold.

The newcomer didn't even bother trying the doorknob. One sharp kick sent the door crashing inward.

A man stepped into the doorway, his silhouette unfamiliar, a gun in his hand. Obviously not Jake.

Her pathetic little lamp would be no match for the gun. The only thing it could do for her—

She threw it, aiming for his head.

He ducked at the last possible moment. The lamp sailed over his shoulder.

She barely noticed the crash as he moved all the way into the room, allowing her to see him fully. He was big and muscular, dressed in jeans and a black T-shirt. A ski mask covered his face, revealing only icy-blue eyes. They seemed to bore into her.

He jerked his head toward the open door. "Come on. Let's go."

"I'm not going anywhere with you."

He whipped the gun up and aimed it right at her face. Even though she'd suspected it was coming, she still flinched when it happened. Terror ripped through her, causing her heart to come to a dead stop in her chest. She'd written this moment before, countless times, scenes where Brock Marshall or some victim about to meet a probable end find themselves staring down the barrel of a gun.

Faced with it for the first time herself, she knew without a doubt that she'd never managed to capture just how terrifying the experience truly was.

Her eyes were pinned so firmly on the gun that she couldn't have moved them if she tried. She felt no relief as it moved to her shoulder, then swung down to her leg.

"We were prepared to carry you once and we'll do it now if we have to. But I bet you'd like it even more than we would if you walked out of here on your own two feet."

If there'd been any question who he was, his words certainly erased it. He was one of the people who'd broken in to her house. And he'd finally caught her defenseless.

His stare was cold and emotionless. She had no doubt his wasn't an empty threat. He might not kill her here, but he wouldn't hesitate to put bullets in a few strategic, non-vital places.

"Why are you doing this?" she whispered, her voice raw.

His expression never wavered in the face of her fear. No sympathy. No pity. Nothing.

"Move," he ordered with another jerk of his head.

Numb, anxiously trying to formulate some kind of plan, Sara obeyed, slowly shuffling around him to the door. She was tempted to go for the gun. As though reading her thoughts, the man moved in tandem with her, mirroring her motions to keep out of her reach as she moved past him, so she preceded him out the door.

Another man stood outside, waiting, a gun in his hands.

As she stepped through the doorway, she immediately glanced in every direction, desperate for some sign of Jake.

Her heart slammed against her chest wall at the sight of a body lying spread-eagle on the ground, covered in blood. The face was nearly obliterated.

Then it sank in. The body wasn't big enough to be Jake. The clothes weren't what she'd seen him wearing just five minutes earlier.

No, it was Roger Halloran, she thought numbly, finally recognizing the shape of the body and the familiar shirt he had worn before. He must have found her and Jake first. He'd led the men here. And paid for it.

But Jake—

There was nothing. Only the rental car sitting where he'd parked it yesterday, Halloran's sedan behind it, and a van—no doubt her captors'—with its sliding door open before her.

A sudden sharp hope pierced her tension. There really was nothing. No body. No blood beyond that which was pooled around Halloran's body.

Which meant there was a chance he'd gotten away.

Despite her current situation, a relieved breath wheezed from her lungs.

He'd gotten away. He must have.

She wouldn't let herself believe otherwise.

She must have come to a stop, because the man behind her poked his gun into her back, prodding her forward.

"Okay, okay," she said, raising her voice. "I'm going."

Newfound optimism rushed through her. They hadn't gotten Jake. He'd gotten away, might even be readying himself to come after them.

And even if he wasn't, if he'd gotten away, then she could, too.

SARA.

Jake was almost to the top of the ravine when he heard her voice. She was close. From her tone, they had her.

Fresh determination filled his veins, giving him the energy to climb the last few feet.

His head had nearly cleared the top when the sound of a door sliding shut reached him.

The van.

Gripping the vines tightly, he raised his head just enough to see over the edge, not wanting to draw the men's attention.

Another door slammed shut, maybe the driver if the second man had gotten in the back with Sara. Moments later, the van's engine roared to life.

Sweat streaming down his face and back, Jake forced himself to wait as the van completed a U-turn and headed down the driveway.

As soon as it was out of view, he launched himself up and over the edge, falling back onto even ground. He didn't let himself slow or give his body time to recover from the climb. Pushing to his feet, he raced back to the cabin, needing his keys. He scooped up both them and his cell phone, then sped to the rental car. Halloran's body lay a few feet away. He ignored it. As far as he could tell, Sara's abductors hadn't done anything to the rental. The tires were still intact. The body looked the same. They probably figured they didn't have to worry about him, so there was no need to take care of his car.

Sloppy of them, but he wasn't going to complain.

Climbing in, he started the engine and pulled forward, executing a turn to avoid Halloran's car. Seconds later he steered the rental car down the long road.

Stopping at the bottom, he quickly checked in both directions. The back of the van was just disappearing around the bend on his right.

He pulled right, trying to gauge how fast to go. He couldn't let the van get too far ahead, but he couldn't follow too closely, either, couldn't let them know he was behind them. As far as he could remember, there weren't too many roads they could turn onto from this one, at least until they reached the highway. So there was less of a risk of losing them along this stretch. Any risk was unacceptable.

Grabbing his cell, he quickly turned it on. There was no use worrying about Sara's abductors using it to track their location now, and he'd need it to call the police as soon as he knew where they were going.

Cold resolve pounding through him, he never took his eyes off the van in front of him. There was no way he was losing Sara, in any respect.

SARA SUCKED IN A BREATH through her teeth. The pain in her belly was growing in intensity.

Rubbing against the ache, she tried to ignore it and focus on the other, more pressing matter at hand.

They were heading back toward Boston. She recognized that much. If that was their ultimate destination, it would take them a while to get there, and she had to make the most of every passing moment to formulate a plan.

Both the driver and the man sitting beside her had removed their ski masks. She suspected they didn't want to draw undue attention from a passing cop, who might question why the driver and one passenger were wearing ski masks and try to pull them over. The action only raised her tension. Even if she hadn't already known they had no intention of letting her survive, the fact that they'd allowed her to see their faces confirmed it.

She guessed they both were in their early thirties, with the same pale blond hair, weak chins and beady eyes. They had to be related, brothers most likely. Neither looked like the kind of man she would have wanted to encounter alone on the street late at night, let alone both of them together.

The driver pulled out a cell phone and hit a couple of buttons before lifting it to his ear. After a few moments he spoke. "It's me. We have her. We're on our way back now."

Three people, Sara thought. There'd been three people at her house, yet there were only two here now. Someone was missing. That was why they'd wanted her to walk to the van rather than carry her, as they no doubt would have if she hadn't scared them off that night. But who was the third? Another stranger? Someone she might know?

She shoved the thought aside. That was the least of her concerns at the moment.

"We took care of them both." The driver responded to something the person on the other end of the line must have said. "They won't be a problem."

Jake and Halloran. That was who he meant. Well, they may have taken care of Halloran, but not Jake, she thought stubbornly, not about to relinquish that desperate belief.

"Okay, see you there," the driver was saying. The words were barely out of his mouth before he pulled the phone away from his ear and ended the call, tossing the phone onto the passenger seat beside him.

Sara tracked its progress with her eyes, not moving a muscle. She doubted there was any chance she could lunge for it or have any hope of getting a call out before they stopped her, but its location was a good thing to know.

"He's meeting us at the house?" the man beside her asked.

"Yeah," the driver said.

"Good." The other man shot her a look that nearly had her recoiling against the window. "It's about time we finished this."

Her skin crawling under the force of his gaze, Sara turned her attention out the window.

Cars flew by traveling in the opposite direction. Unfamiliar scenery whipped past. She was quickly losing her bearings as they whisked her to an unknown destination, an uncertain fate.

What would Brock Marshall do?

The question echoed distantly in her mind. No answers were forthcoming. She might instinctively know what the hero of her stories should do in any situation, but she had no idea what to do in her own.

What she wouldn't give for the safety of her fictionalized world, where everything happened according to her dictates and she knew all would end well because she made it so.

But this was real. Nine months ago she'd stepped out of the safe, comfortable confines of her stories and into reality and there was no going back. There were no guarantees here.

The sole similarity between her stories and her current situation was that any hope of everything turning out well lay entirely within her hands.

JAKE FOLLOWED SEVERAL CAR lengths behind the van, what he considered a safe distance. After the first few miles he'd stopped worrying that they would try to lose him. They'd given no indication they'd known he was there. They might not even be keeping too close a watch behind them, not expecting anyone to follow. He wondered if they'd even looked at the rental car back at the cabin. Most likely Halloran's sedan had partially blocked it from view when they pulled up. And after they thought they'd taken care of him, there was no reason to bother.

He might not have to worry about them trying to lose him, but he did have to worry about losing them just the same. The cell phone sat on the panel beside him. The tension gripping him kept him from reaching for it.

He couldn't take his hands off the steering wheel, couldn't take his eyes off the road, couldn't do anything that might cause him to lose sight of the van, of Sara, for even a second.

Even if he could contact someone, who would it be? The state police? Somebody local? He didn't know this area well enough, didn't even know where the hell he was.

So he did the only thing he could. He followed.

SARA HAD NO IDEA where they were. They'd pulled off the highway long before they made it to Boston, traveling through a few small towns and down long stretches of road until she was hopelessly lost.

Not that she was in any particular hurry to reach their destination, knowing what they had in mind for her. But if—no, *when*—she managed to get away, she likely would have to run. A difficult enough proposition given the pain searing through her and the added weight she was carrying. A near futile one if she didn't know where she was or where she could run to.

Suddenly, with no warning whatsoever, the driver turned the van into the trees lining the road. More specifically, another road, one she hadn't even realized was there, cut between the trees.

The foliage cleared on the other side, revealing a large plot of land. A long driveway led to a big, two-story house sitting alone in the middle of the lot bordered by trees. As they came closer, Sara could see just how run-down the place was. The house appeared to be at least a century old, its paint fading and peeling, some of the old-fashioned window shutters hanging loose. The grass all around it was overgrown, bearing more of a resemblance to a farmer's field than a lawn.

A chill trickled down Sara's spine. The house was completely isolated. The property vast enough that no one on the other side of the trees in any direction would likely have any idea what was happening here.

Like where they brought pregnant girls to live out their pregnancies, and no one would ever know?

Was this where they'd been kept? Had they come here by choice, under the impression this was a sanctuary? Had their initial glimpse of the decaying structure killed that hope right away? Or had they been drugged when they arrived, brought inside against their will? No doubt that would have been easier to accomplish with the girls relatively early in their pregnancies.

The van pulled around the back of the house and came to a stop next to a door. Cutting the engine, the driver climbed out and came around the side to pull the sliding door open. The man sitting next to her climbed out, then motioned to her with his gun. "Get out."

She considered refusing, but that seemed unlikely to accomplish much. At this point, it would probably be easy for them to drug her and carry her inside. She couldn't let that happen. Her only chance of getting out of this was to stay alert.

The thug grabbed her arm as soon as she stepped out of the van and prodded her forward. The other man had the door to the house open. She slowly shuffled through it, trying to take all the time she could to get her bearings and figure a way out of this.

The house was eerily silent as they entered. The kitchen appeared to have been frozen in the 1960s. The appliances were all several decades old, the style of the furniture, right down to the ancient clock on the wall, severely out-of-date.

Sara barely had time to take in the scene when she felt the gun at her back, nudging her toward another doorway across the room. It opened onto two hallways, one leading directly in front of her toward what looked like the front door, the other leading right and down the length of the house.

"Right," the man behind her ordered.

She obeyed, stumbling down the hall to where a door at the end lay open. The room within was clearly set up for a medical procedure. A couple of metal poles, the kind used to hang IVs, bracketed the bed in the center of the room. The bed itself was covered with only a fitted sheet on the mattress, a few pillows tossed haphazardly against the headboard. A layer of plastic was laid down on the hardwood floor. To make the cleanup from the anticipated mess easier.

Terror squeezing her throat, she whipped around, reaching for the door. If she could slam it in their faces—

She didn't get the chance. The man right behind her slapped his palm against the surface, holding it back, his lip curling in a sneer as he stepped through the doorway.

Sara stumbled backward, away from them, farther into the room. She jerked her head from side to side, seeking any exit. The door they'd entered appeared to be the only one leading in or out of the room. There was a window on each of the side walls. She slowly inched toward the closest one without looking at it, weighing her chances of getting through it. They didn't look good. Even if she was capable of climbing out a window in her condition—and she could hardly imagine how she'd hoist herself over the ledge—she'd have to get it open first. And they'd stop her before she managed it.

No, the only real way out was back through the door.

She would have to get past them.

Easier said than done when the one man still had his gun in his hand. Maybe she should be grateful he hadn't already shot her in the leg to keep her from getting away. Maybe he just didn't want to deal with the mess, already expecting to have to take care of enough of one in the near future.

The other man, the driver, didn't have anything in his hands. She had no doubt he had a weapon, perhaps tucked into the back of his pants. He didn't look at her as he moved to another door on the left. She didn't see where he'd gone at first, her eyes widening as they took in the dresser he passed on his way.

Syringes and ominous-looking little vials were lined up on the top of the dresser.

Her heartbeat kicking up a notch, she jerked her gaze back to the man who remained in the room. He was staring at her, a smirk on his face, his eyes dead.

The other man reentered the room out of the edge of her vision. She finally saw that he'd stepped into a bathroom. He was drying his hands on a towel as he returned. "Let's do this," he said.

Before anyone could respond to the statement, a sound met their ears. A door slamming open down the hall. Both men whipped their heads to the noise.

"Help!" she screamed, the instinct automatic, hoping against hope it was someone she could trust, even as a voice in the back of her mind told her it had to be the anticipated third member of their group.

As though confirming it, neither man looked the slightest bit perturbed at her outburst.

The man who'd driven fluttered a hand toward the door. "Go ahead. I can handle this."

The other man shot her a look of sheer contempt as he moved away and headed for the exit, pulling the door shut behind him.

Even as the door closed, she focused all her attention on the man before her. She didn't bother to be offended that he'd dismissed his partner so casually. Two against one were hardly fair odds. One on one at least gave her more of a fighting chance, especially since he didn't seem to have a weapon. He continued to dry his hands, finally raising dead eyes to meet hers.

"Now, Sara, I'm going to ask you to get on the bed."

She had no trouble recognizing that voice. "You were at my house. You're the man with the syringe."

"I'm flattered you remember me," he said, though his expression said he was anything but pleased.

"What are you, a doctor?"

"Close enough."

Close enough to deliver a healthy baby when the mother's survival wasn't an issue, she thought with a shudder. How many babies had been born, how many young women had died, in this house, in this very room? "I didn't know doctors made house calls anymore."

"Most people can be convinced to do anything for the right price."

"And what's your price, Doctor? Maybe I can match it."

"Doubtful. I'm satisfied with my current arrangement. Now, why don't you get on the bed?"

"Why don't you go to hell?"

He opened his mouth to reply. Nothing came out. Instead, his eyes suddenly widened, his gaze dropping to her feet.

Adrenaline roaring through her veins, she

didn't even realize what had happened until she glanced down to see the plastic beneath her feet was drenched.

She froze, the shock of it delaying the realization for a split second.

Oh, God. Her water had broken.

She was in labor.

The intermittent pain in her abdomen that she'd attributed to stress and maybe heartburn and had done her best to ignore took on an all new meaning.

Contractions. She was having contractions.

Even as the dazed thought floated through her mind, another pain, so sharp and fierce she couldn't even begin to ignore it, ripped through her. Her vision clouded. A raw scream rose in her throat, instead coming out as a choked whimper as her knees buckled and threatened to give way. She gripped the edge of the bed to stay on her feet.

Through the haze of pain, she saw his face hovering in front of her.

He smiled.

"It hurts, doesn't it?" he asked, false concern dripping from every word as he slowly moved toward her. He picked up a syringe from the dresser and removed the cap.

"Stay away from me," she grunted, the words coming between rapid breaths. She tried to get her feet to move, to inch backward, away from him. She couldn't. It was all she could do to remain standing.

Ignoring her, he pushed the needle into one of the vials of liquid, quickly filling the syringe. "It must be unbearable. Worse than anything I could possibly imagine or hope to endure. You shouldn't have to, either. You *don't* have to."

She wanted to slam her hands over her ears to avoid hearing any more. Gripped with pain, she couldn't do anything but stand there, shoulders hunched, chest heaving, unable to move. She tried to ignore what he was saying, but she couldn't block out the sickly sweet, condescending tone in his voice.

Setting the now-empty vial back on the dresser, he took a step toward her. "I can make the pain go away. All you have to do is get on the bed and I can make the pain stop. You won't have to feel it anymore."

She wouldn't feel *anything* anymore, she thought, knowing exactly what he was thinking. If he got anywhere near her, she'd be put under and never wake up again. They would take her baby and she wouldn't be able to do anything to stop them.

Her baby.

And just like that, she knew, as firmly and undeniably as if there'd never been a doubt in her mind.

This wasn't a stranger's baby. It was hers. And no matter how or why it had come to be, it was here now. And it was *hers*. Hers to care for. Hers to deal with. Hers to defend.

Which was exactly what she had to do.

In front of her, the man moved inexorably closer, his steps unhurried and confident, that smug smile on his face.

Something inside her snapped. She was standing before him, experiencing something worse than anything she'd ever felt in her entire life, and this *man* was *smiling* at her. Not with sympathy. Not with tenderness.

With delight. As though he was enjoying her pain.

In a heartbeat she forgot that pain as something far more powerful exploded in every cell of her being.

Rage.

She threw her mouth open and screamed. She screamed with fury and pain and disgust and determination. Every muddled, conflicting emotion flooding her body came together, surging into one instinct, filling her with power and strength.

She felt a jolt of satisfaction as the man's smile vanished in an instant. He actually took a step back, his eyes widening with alarm.

He hadn't seen anything yet.

She glanced around wildly, her gaze falling on a tall floor lamp a few feet away. She lunged for it, grabbing it tightly with both hands, and swung the base at him.

He lurched backward out of its reach at the last second. Now visibly nervous, the man lifted his hands. All it did was remind her of the syringe poised between his fingers.

"N-now, Sara," he stammered, "you don't want to hurt yourself."

"No, *you* don't want to hurt me," she growled. Not yet. He couldn't, not without risking hurting the baby, not if he wanted to get paid.

He couldn't hurt her.

But she could damn well hurt him.

Chapter Eleven

Jake eased off the gas as the van suddenly executed a turn ahead onto a road he couldn't even see. Once it was out of sight, he counted to five before pushing down on the gas slightly and slowly rolling past the opening in the trees through which the van had disappeared. He hesitated just long enough to take in the long driveway the van had headed up before accelerating further. If he was right, that was the driveway to some kind of structure, most likely a house. There'd been a single small mailbox at the end of the driveway. He couldn't follow any farther in the car. He'd have to walk, remain undetected.

There was a bend in the road ahead. He quickly pulled in behind some shrubbery, barely high enough to hide the car, and parked.

He was halfway out of the vehicle when he remembered his cell phone. He could call for help. The problem was, he had no idea where to send them.

The hell with it. He scooped up the phone and punched in the digits as he made his way back to the driveway.

"9-1-1. What's your emergency?"

"A woman has been kidnapped. I followed them to where they brought her. I need the police here *now,* before they hurt her."

"Sir, I'm going to need you to stay calm. You say a woman has been kidnapped—"

"She's eight and a half months pregnant. I don't know where we are. It's a big old house in the middle of nowhere. There's a black mailbox at the end of the driveway with the number 827 on it. Does that mean anything to you?"

A beat of silence came across the line, either because the person on the other end didn't know how to deal with this bizarre caller or because the description did mean something to him.

Either way, Jake couldn't wait and see.

"Listen, if it does mean something to you, I need you to send somebody. The lives of a woman and her baby are at stake. If not, maybe you can trace this call. Hurry."

"Sir—"

Without disconnecting the call, Jake

dropped the phone, leaving the line open. He didn't know if it was necessary for a trace, but he wasn't going to take any chances. He only hoped they took the call seriously.

In the meantime, he had to do something. Just like that first night when he'd heard gunfire in Sara's house, there was no way he was going to wait outside when she might be dead before the police arrived.

He had to get to the house.

Trees bordered the driveway on the right. Weapon in hand, he stayed close to them, hoping that no one within the house saw his approach. He had a feeling the people who'd brought Sara here would be too occupied with her to notice any unexpected visitors. That just left anyone else who might be in the building. There could be a security system of some kind, but judging from the state of this place, he doubted it. He scanned the perimeter and didn't see any cameras or wires overhead leading from the house outward.

He was halfway to the house when the sound of an engine reached his ears. He quickly ducked into the trees, and seconds later, watched a car roar by on its way up the driveway, kicking up a cloud of dust in its wake. He didn't recognize the vehicle, couldn't see the driver.

As he approached the building, he didn't see either the car or the van. The drivers must have pulled around the back of the house. Sure enough, making his way to the rear of the structure, he found both the van and a beat-up, old compact parked next to the back door. Both vehicles appeared to be empty.

He approached the house carefully, listening for the sound of voices as he darted from the trees to the side of the building. There was a door to the house directly on the other side of the van. He moved along the back of the house toward it, ducking low to avoid the windows as best as possible, giving quick peeks inside as he passed. Bracing his back against the wall, he took a deep breath before slowly peering through the window in the door.

It led into a kitchen. The room was empty.

Reassured, he carefully eased the door open, painfully aware a telltale creak or squeal could betray him at any moment. Moving with painstaking slowness, he slid through the minimal space he created.

Voices drifted toward him from an opening across the room. Inching forward, he made his way toward it, then followed the voices down the hallway to the right, listening carefully to gauge how many there were and whether the speakers were armed.

"Do you realize how many risks we've taken in the last three days to get this woman?" a man said from the closest opening to his left.

"It wouldn't have been a problem if you'd bothered to find out she had a gun in the first place," a second voice responded. "All this could have been taken care of days ago."

That voice. Male. Jake instantly felt the flash of recognition. He'd heard that voice before, and recently.

"It's not my fault she's a damn shut-in who didn't leave the house long enough for me to do a proper search. You're the one who said this job would be a piece of cake. One last easy score before we're done with this."

"And it should have been."

"Whatever. This is it. Tommy and I made up our minds. The money's not worth it. We're out after this. It's over."

"You're right. It is."

Jake was familiar enough with the sound of a bullet fired from a silenced weapon. He'd heard it up close and personal just two days earlier when he'd tackled the intruder who'd broken in to his house. So he immediately knew what the muffled noise was, and understood the significance of the sound of something heavy crashing to the floor seconds later.

Quiet resounded in the aftermath of the shooting. Jake slowly counted to ten, then carefully peered around the corner, his weapon half raised.

A man in a faded black T-shirt and worn jeans stood in the hallway with his back to him. Even from behind, Jake had no trouble recognizing him.

Just as Jake made the ID, Noah Brooks whirled around, already raising his gun. Jake barely managed to duck back around the corner before Noah got off a shot. The bullet whizzed past where he'd been standing to land in the wall in front of him.

"Who's there?" Brooks demanded.

Jake said nothing. Answering would offer him no advantage. But if he remained quiet, the other man might come to investigate, maybe just to make sure there was even someone there. Then Jake could get the drop on him.

"I got a good enough look to see it's Armstrong, isn't it?" Brooks continued. "Were they stupid enough to let you follow them here?"

Jake breathed in and out slowly, careful not to move a muscle or make a single sound.

He was tempted to retreat, see if Sara was elsewhere in the house. But if he stepped wrong, the man could come after him, take him out if Jake didn't get him first. Not to mention he didn't know who else was here. Brooks had said there were three of them—himself, the dead man and one other. The last was probably with Sara, unless there was someone else. Even if there wasn't, he couldn't count on the man staying with Sara. Hell, maybe he didn't want him to.

"I know you're there," Noah said pleasantly. Jake could practically picture that same smile he'd offered them yesterday on the man's face at that very moment. "I'm assuming you're armed, and you already know I am. I can wait you out as long as I have to. I'm in no hurry. I'm just waiting for a baby to be born. You're the one with the time crunch. You want to get to Sara, don't you? So why don't you come out here and we can settle this."

The bastard was right. He didn't have time to waste in a standoff. He needed to eliminate the threat this man posed. "What are you suggesting?" he said finally. "A shoot-out?"

"You could always come out and we could talk."

His voice had a cool, calm tone Jake guessed served him well in his role as a teen counselor. "And I'm supposed to believe you won't shoot me?"

"You could try trusting me."

Jake decided he had to keep the man talking. Until he figured out a way to get past him, he needed to know his location. "Kind of hard to trust someone who just murdered his business partner. Someone who's been doing what you've been doing to those pregnant girls." Disgust surged from his gut. "You were supposed to *help* them."

"I did help them. I helped them provide their children with better lives than sluts like them could ever dream of giving them. And at the same time I helped every other kid who needs the youth center."

The words stopped Jake cold. The youth center... He remembered Sara's belief that Brooks wasn't involved because he didn't even have enough money for a pair of shoes that weren't falling apart. But he also remembered the man saying how much the youth center meant to him. Was it possible this really had nothing to do with personal profit?

Those anonymous donations Noah had mentioned to Kendra—funds from the sale of the girls' babies?

"Is all this just to raise money for the youth center?" he asked, unable to keep the disbelief from his voice.

"The center provides a vital service for the kids who need it," Brooks replied, his voice taking on a disturbing intensity. "There's never enough money. I found a way to increase donations in a way that best serves everyone."

"Not the girls."

"They got what they deserved. They should have thought twice before sleeping around. Can you believe most of them wanted to keep their babies, actually thought they could be mothers to them?" He barked out a laugh. "Stupid sluts. It takes more to be a mother than the ability to spread your legs."

Even after knowing everything the man had done, the viciousness in his voice still managed to catch Jake by surprise. Noah was raised by a single mother, he'd said. A mother who'd been an unwed teenager? The sheer hatred in his voice had to be coming from somewhere.

Jake shot a glance behind him, not wanting to leave his back completely open. "What about Mark? Was he a part of this?"

"No. He didn't figure it out until after Kendra forced him out at the center."

Jake couldn't help but feel relieved for

Sara's sake. Now he just had to make sure she learned the truth.

"I bet he started thinking about how likely it would be that pregnant girls would go missing from the same youth center employing the son of a woman who went to prison for selling the babies of pregnant teens. If it wasn't him, then chances were it had to be someone who knew the story, someone who'd taken it as inspiration to do the same." Sara had been right. It was too much of a coincidence. But there was an explanation. "Kendra said you and Mark were good friends. Good enough that he felt comfortable telling you about his past?"

"We grabbed a drink after work a few times. He was very sympathetic when I told him about my terrible mother. I was very sympathetic when he told me about his."

"And then you took advantage of what he told you to relaunch his mother's business."

"It seemed an ideal solution for everybody. The center benefits, the rest of the kids benefit, both the babies and people looking to adopt benefit."

Damn it, the man just wasn't moving. If Jake estimated where he was standing, based both on the sound of his voice and where he'd been when Jake last saw him, he might be able to give off a shot. But if he only had one shot he wanted to be sure.

"How'd you know about Sara?"

"The last time I saw him, I could tell Mark was starting to suspect me. So I had Johnny here keep an eye on him. At first I wanted to know who she was. Mark wasn't the one-night-stand type. I thought she had to be somebody important, especially if he was sleeping with her. Maybe somebody he'd shared his suspicions with. I didn't realize Mark *was* the one-night-stand type after all."

Or maybe he hadn't been. Maybe he'd just been a man who'd lost everything, Jake thought as recognition shafted through him, looking for one night of comfort in a woman's arms.

"And then you found out she was pregnant."

"We were watching her, trying to figure out if Mark had told her anything that night that might point to us, to see if she needed to be eliminated. We were watching when she went to the doctor, and we were watching when she bought prenatal vitamins."

"Eliminated," Jake echoed. "Eliminated like Mark?"

"He'd put too much together," Brooks said simply. "He'd started looking into my background. It was only a matter of time before he found out about this place."

And if Mark had found out about this place, he would have found some of the girls still alive. So they'd run him down in the street. "Why come after Sara now?"

"Because of the budget shortfall caused by the funds we lost due to the bad press."

"Which you caused in the first place."

"All the more reason for me to be the one to replace them."

"Which meant finding a baby to sell." And he just happened to know of a pregnant woman, one he'd already investigated well enough to know she didn't have anyone in her life, no close family, no close friends. Seemingly no one to care if she and her baby disappeared without a trace. Which was exactly what might have happened if she hadn't had her gun that night. Which was what still might happen.

"Mark cared a great deal about the center and the kids there. It only seems right that he be able to provide one last gift to it."

The lack of guilt, of doubt in his voice only fueled Jake's anger. The bastard sounded as if he truly believed every word. The scary thing was, he probably did.

"Nothing about this is *right*," Jake growled.

Whatever response Brooks might have made was cut off by the sound of a woman's scream.

Sara.

The shock of it, the sudden terror that gripped him, made Jake freeze.

The scream had come from just down the hall. She was only a few yards away. God only knew what they were doing to her, while he was stuck here, with Brooks standing between them.

"Ouch," Brooks said, his voice rich with sarcasm. "That was worse than the last one. Sounds like it hurts."

Furious, Jake took an automatic step, then stopped, weighing his chances of getting past the doorway. They weren't good. He didn't doubt Brooks would open fire at the first sign of movement in the doorway. Even if he lunged across the opening, he might not be fast enough to avoid a bullet. And if he did, Brooks would definitely come after him to keep him from getting to Sara, from interfering with whatever they were doing to her.

As though reading his mind, Brooks said, "Go ahead. I'm sure you want to make a break for it. Let's see if you can outrun a bullet on that bad knee of yours. Hell, what if I didn't even hit anything vital? What if I hit your knee?" He laughed. "Wouldn't that be ironic?"

The man's words, the idea of a bullet tearing through the tattered remains of his surgically repaired knee, made him freeze.

But though the significance of it wouldn't hit him until later, his first thought wasn't that he'd never get back on the field or play again if this man shot him.

It was that he wouldn't be able to get to Sara and the baby. He'd go down, making an easy target if he couldn't get his weapon up in time.

No. That wasn't an option. He had to get to her.

He thought quickly, seeking another option. From what he'd seen, Brooks was standing in what appeared to be a living room. A room like that wouldn't have a doorway into a rear hallway its sole entrance point. No, there had to be another, more prominent one. Probably down the other hall he'd seen when he'd followed the voices into this one, the one leading toward the front of the house.

Again entirely too aware of the possibility of making the wrong sound, he began to creep backward, toward the corner, toward the other hall. Despite the logic of the choice, his instincts rebelled at the idea of moving away from where Sara was. He pushed back the thoughts. He had no choice. He had to take this chance. It was the only one he had.

"Armstrong?"

Brooks's voice wafted toward him as he turned the corner into the other hallway. Sure enough, there was an opening up ahead to the right. He heard the voice coming from both behind and in front of him.

He made his way to the entryway just as Brooks called again.

"Armstrong!"

The fury in the man's voice told Jake two things. Brooks was losing it, and he was heading away from his current position.

Slowly, carefully, Jake ventured a glance into the room.

Brooks was inching toward the opening to the hallway Jake had just vacated.

Taking a step into the doorway, Jake raised his weapon.

Then, just as he took aim, Brooks seemed to realize his mistake.

He started to whirl around.

Too late.

Jake fired, hitting Brooks's right shoulder. A screech of pain filled the air, the weapon flying out of the man's hand.

Jake instantly lowered his weapon, taking aim again. He took the shot.

Brooks screamed again as the bullet landed in his right thigh. Even as he started to crumple, Jake shifted his aim to the other thigh and fired. Killing him was too good for the bastard, but he wasn't about to let him get in his way.

Jake's aim was true. Brooks fell to the floor, his yelps giving way to a steady stream of curses. "You son of a bitch!"

"Back at you," Jake spat, already halfway across the room, dodging the first body on the floor, then Brooks. Ignoring the man's screams, he kicked Brooks's weapon into the hallway, then farther down the corridor in the direction he was heading. Anything to keep it out of Brooks's reach, even if he didn't look to be in any shape to go for it.

Even before he landed the second kick, he'd already forgotten the gun. He rushed down the hall, slamming doors open, checking each one, finally arriving at the end. One last door.

He threw it open.

The first thing he saw was the blood, a swath of it spread across what appeared to be plastic laid down on the wooden floorboards. His heart came to a dead stop in his chest as his gaze followed the trail of redness. But it didn't lead to Sara. A man lay facedown a few feet away, the blood spreading from his body.

He took a tentative step into the room and peered around the bed in the center.

And then he saw her.

She was sitting on the floor, leaning against the wall in the far corner of the room. Her damp hair was plastered to her scalp and face. And in her arms she held the baby.

Still terrified, he moved closer, avoiding the blood on the floor, scanning every inch of the pair in the corner. As though sensing his presence, she lifted her head. Her eyes were glassy and shell-shocked. It took a second, but then she seemed to recognize him. She relaxed almost imperceptibly, returning the arm back to the baby.

He stared transfixed at the child. It was covered in gunk, but the baby was moving its head and making gurgling sounds. The umbilical cord was still attached. That was weird. He was no expert, but he would have thought the doctor would have cleaned it up before giving it to her.

Except the doctor wouldn't have given it to her, he realized. They'd wanted to take it from her. He shot a startled glance at the man slumped on the ground a few feet away and realized there was only one way she could still have the baby.

Feeling as dazed as she looked, he slowly crouched in front of her. "My God. Did you do this by yourself?"

She stared back at him, unblinking, her face wet with tears. "I couldn't let them take my baby."

The words came out in a hoarse whisper, but there was no mistaking the firm fierceness in them. In spite of everything, a gentle smile pulled at one corner of his mouth. "Your baby, huh?"

She raised her chin, her arm tensing around the child. Protective. Possessive. "Yeah."

He reached out and wiped a tear away with his thumb. "Come on. Let's get you out of here."

She gave her head a furious shake when he moved to pick her up. "Don't. I'm too heavy."

"No, you're not." Before she could say another word, he lifted the two of them into his arms and rose to his feet. The distant echo of sirens reached them from outside. The police, and hopefully an ambulance. Just in the nick of time.

Sara released a soft sigh and dropped her

head against his shoulder. This time it was he who tightened his grasp, around her and her baby, safe in his arms, as he carried them out of the house and into the light of day.

Chapter Twelve

Sara had just woken from a brief nap when a quiet knock drew her attention to the door of her hospital room. Expecting Jake or one of the nurses bringing the baby back, she was already starting to smile as she turned her head in that direction.

Instead, Detective Bates stood in the open doorway. "Ms. Carson," he acknowledged with a nod.

"Detective Bates," she returned, unable to hide her surprise. She scooted up in bed a little, then winced as a twinge struck her. Two days later and she was still sore. "What brings you here?"

He stepped into the room and slowly moved toward the bed. "I drove up as soon as I heard what happened."

"This is a little out of your jurisdiction, isn't it?"

"The girls disappeared in my jurisdiction, so I go wherever the case takes me. Even if it didn't, I'd still be here. I figure Halloran deserved that much."

"I'm sure he would have appreciated it," Sara said, keeping her tone neutral. She was hardly the right person to comment on what Halloran deserved. The memory of the trouble he'd caused was still too fresh in her mind.

Her perspective had changed slightly in the past few days, now that she knew what it was to hold her baby in her arms. Her child, the son she'd named Daniel Mark Carson, was only two days old, yet she'd already known the terror of what it would be like to lose him. A part of her could understand Halloran's motivations in a way she hadn't before. The rest of her wasn't ready to simply excuse his actions as a result.

"I just wanted to check in on you," Bates said gruffly. "I thought you might like an update on the case and everything that's come out. The locals didn't look like they were in a big hurry to talk to you about it, but I figured you deserved that much."

"Oh," she said, surprised again. "Thank you." She glanced around, trying to figure out how long Jake had been gone and whether she should ask Bates to wait. She'd known Jake was going to grab something to eat, but couldn't remember how long ago that had been. She already missed him; he'd barely left her side since he'd carried her out of the house where she'd given birth.

Before she had the chance to say anything, Bates started speaking again. "Anyway, McCoy's been talking."

Sara suppressed a shudder. Tommy McCoy, she now knew, was the man who'd intended to deliver her baby, the one she'd managed to fight off. His partner in her abduction from the cabin had been his brother, Johnny. Both men were Noah Brooks's second cousins. "What's he saying?"

"He's selling out Brooks. When he learned that Brooks killed his brother, he couldn't cut a deal fast enough."

"So he confessed to everything?"

"Put it in writing and all. How much do you know already?"

"Jake told me what Noah confessed to him, but it wasn't much. Just that he did it to raise money for the youth center, and apparently had serious issues with his mother."

"I'm not surprised. She was fifteen when she had him, apparently forced into keeping him by her parents. She was seriously abusive toward him for much of his child-hood, right up until the time she died in a fall at the family home when he was fourteen—which no longer seems like the accident it was deemed at the time. Even beyond his mother, it doesn't sound like his family life was much to speak of."

"That's what I heard." So Noah had been honest about that much at least. The local police had told her yesterday that the Brooks clan was notorious enough around there that when Jake told the emergency dispatcher the number of the house he'd followed her ab-ductors to, the man had been familiar enough with both the property and the family that he'd wasted no time sending someone out to investigate.

"Both McCoy brothers were especially nasty types, with extensive criminal records," Bates continued. "When Brooks needed someone to help him implement his plan, they were the obvious choices for him to go to. Tommy McCoy used to be a para-medic, until a drug habit cost him his job, which is how he had enough medical knowl-edge to tend to the pregnant girls and deliver their babies. Johnny was in charge of keeping Tommy clean long enough to take care of the girls. Both brothers had enough

contact with numerous shady lawyers—
thanks to their pasts—to know who might be
able to help them. They hooked Brooks up
with a lawyer who set up the adoption side
of the business as well as the bank accounts
through which Brooks funneled his share of
the money back into the youth center in the
form of anonymous donations.

"You probably already figured out that
they kept the missing girls at the house,
sedated until they reached full term." Sara
nodded. "The bodies were buried in the
backyard, all of them wrapped in the same
type of plastic that had been laid down in the
room where you gave birth."

"How tidy of them," she said darkly. "Why
did they wait so long to come after me?"

"After the missing girls were connected to
the center, the McCoys wanted out. They
didn't want to get caught, so they...finished
with the last girl they had and pretty much
closed up shop. A month or so ago, Brooks
finally talked them into going after you as
one last score, just because you seemed like
an easy mark. The real reason is that the
youth center was especially cash-strapped,
so he needed money fast. He's not talking,
but we're thinking that's why he killed
Johnny McCoy. He didn't need him any-

more, and fewer partners would mean fewer shares to be split. He likely meant to kill Tommy McCoy once he delivered your baby, then would have taken it to the lawyer himself."

"But I wasn't an easy mark. Why'd they keep coming after me?"

"They knew Kendall had—"

"Williams," Sara interrupted, feeling an unexpected surge of protectiveness. "I'm pretty sure he would rather have been called Mark Williams."

"Williams, then," Bates said. "They knew Williams had been drinking the night you met him, and the two of you talked for a while at the bar. They didn't know what he might have told you. At first it seemed like you didn't know anything, but then you met Halloran after their first attempt to take you and found out about Williams and the center. They were afraid you might remember something he'd told you, something that might not have meant something to you until you learned more about the situation. That gave them an extra reason to take care of you. At least, that's the line Brooks fed the McCoys. I don't know if he believed it, but they seemed to buy it."

"So who killed Mark?"

"Johnny McCoy was behind the wheel but Tommy's claiming it was all Brooks's idea. I'm betting it's something they all decided on. They all knew he was looking into Brooks's background. They had to stop him before he took his suspicions to the police."

"Did he say how they got into my house?"

"Johnny McCoy swiped your keys out of your purse when you were at the grocery store one day, made an impression with putty or wax, then returned the keys before you even noticed."

So it had been that easy. She shook her head. "Was anyone else from the center involved?"

"It doesn't look like it. McCoy didn't name anybody else and didn't seem to recognize the names of any of the other staff members when questioned. There was nothing in the house or Brooks's apartment to connect anyone else to any of this. It really appears that this was a four-person operation."

Four people. Noah, the two McCoys and the attorney. Despite her worries about a vast conspiracy, it really had come down to just four people. And almost more important than the four names on the list was the one that wasn't.

Though Jake had already confirmed it for her, soon the rest of the world would know.

Mark had been innocent.

In the back of her mind, Sara registered Bates starting to describe the efforts to track down the adopted babies. Her thoughts were already drifting away, to the man she'd known for such a brief time, who'd changed her life forever. There had been several times over the past few days when she'd thought of him, when she'd held Danny in her arms and thought of the father he would never know. Her memories of Mark were no longer tinged with unease, but with sadness. Now that she knew the truth, it seemed clear he'd spent his life trying to do the right thing and make up for his mother's crimes. Naturally it had led to his counseling work at the youth center. She could only imagine the guilt he must have felt when he realized that he'd inadvertently led to Noah's actions, perpetuating the very deeds he'd been trying to make amends for.

A small part of her did wonder why he'd spent the night with her. Maybe he'd recognized some sadness in her that matched what he was feeling; maybe he'd just wanted to forget everything for one night; maybe he just hadn't wanted to be alone, either, and she'd been there at the right moment. She remembered that first look they'd shared, the smile she'd considered almost tentative. With what she now knew, she wondered if he hadn't been sure what her response would be, if after being viewed with suspicion—including the suspicion of those he'd considered his closest friends—he'd grown unused to anyone looking at him without it. Whatever the reason, her pregnancy hadn't been the result of some plot. It had been an accident after all.

Just a few days ago the knowledge would have meant the world to her. Now she understood just how little it really mattered. However it had happened, she'd already come to terms with the result. That was what counted. Still, she was glad for the baby's sake. Someday he would want to know about the man whose blood ran through his veins and what kind of person he'd been. She would at least be able to tell him he really had been a decent man. A nice guy, as she'd thought. It seemed her instincts hadn't been completely off. She had known a good man when she'd found one.

The sound of footsteps drew her eye to the door in time to see Jake enter. He stopped in the doorway, his eyes going first to her, then scanning the room, his gaze alert, his stance protective.

Yes, she thought as she drank in the sight of him, her heart leaping into her throat and happiness flooding her veins. She did know a good man when she found one.

Epilogue

Sara stared at her reflection in her bedroom mirror, trying to calm the butterflies fluttering in her stomach.

This was it. Tonight was the night.

It hardly seemed like something to be nervous about, especially compared with everything she'd already been through. The knowledge did nothing to calm her nerves.

It had been only three months since those desperate days leading up to Danny's birth, yet it seemed like a lifetime ago. The time since had become a blur of busy days, sleepless nights, one little baby.

And Jake.

Her lips curved at the very thought of him. He'd been with her every step of the way, by her side every day since she'd left the hospital. After a while he'd been at his house so seldom it seemed natural for him to move into hers. By all rights, they really should be sick of each other by now. Instead, every day seemed to have only brought them closer.

As though conjured by her thoughts, he appeared behind her. He grinned at her, and her smile deepened in response.

She turned to face him. "Everything all locked up?"

"Yep. And the security system's set." They shared a smile over that. Though they had no reason to believe anyone would be coming after her again, one of the first things they'd done was have an alarm system installed in her house. She'd had enough experiences with uninvited nighttime visitors to last her a lifetime.

"I didn't think he'd ever fall asleep."

"Enjoy it while it lasts. Chances are, he'll be up again before long."

"Don't jinx it," he said. "Now you're just asking for trouble."

Sara moved to the bed to pull back the covers. "If I didn't know better I'd think he was trying to play chaperone."

"I think he's a little young to know about stuff like this."

"His little brain's developing all the time. He could be picking things up."

"At three months?"

"We could have a little genius on our hands."

"I wouldn't be surprised."

Pride radiated in his voice, and Sara's smile deepened. It didn't matter that he'd played no part in the baby's conception. He'd been there for not just Danny, but her, every step of the way. Sharing DNA with him couldn't have made him Danny's father any more than he was now.

She could watch the two of them for hours. Something about the sight of those massive hands handling that tiny body with the gentlest of care always made a lump form in her throat. He was a natural with Danny. Despite the fact that he hadn't read any of the books she'd pored over, he seemed to know what to do. As she'd once told him, some things just came naturally.

Maybe he was simply remembering things from his own childhood, which his time with the baby appeared to have brought back to him. He'd been talking more about his brothers, mostly memories of when they'd been boys. She didn't even think he realized he was doing it half the time. They'd be talking about Danny, and Jake would mention something about his own child-hood, with one brother or another coming up often enough that she knew all their names and various things about them. It was clear they were on his mind more and more. He hadn't said anything yet, but she had the feeling he was seriously considering trying to contact them. She hadn't said anything either, even though she thought it was a great idea. She didn't want to push him. She suspected it was only a matter of time.

Meanwhile, he'd made it clear that he'd come to terms with the fact that his football career was over and that he was fine with it. Though she wouldn't have expected it when they first met, Sara believed him. After deciding not to have the surgery, he was exploring several opportunities for the future, but for the time being, they were just enjoying being together, the three of them.

But tonight wasn't about the baby or Jake's family or anything else. It was about the two of them, and finally taking a step that had been delayed for too long.

Even as the thought crossed her mind, another nervous tremor rumbled through her and she swallowed hard.

He must have read her expression. "We don't have to do this if you don't want to," he said.

"No, I want to." She had for a long time

now. Even with all the exhaustion of caring for the baby and trying to get through each day without losing her mind, she'd wanted this, the anticipation carrying her through.

The mere sight of him was enough to make her heart beat faster. Every time he came near or she heard the low rumble of his voice and felt it vibrate through her, tingles erupted along her skin. Whenever they fell asleep and he held her in his arms, the rightness of it threatened to overwhelm her.

But she wanted more. She wanted to be with him. She wanted to make love to him.

Excitement and apprehension warred within her. Because being with him like this would mean finally exposing herself in a way she'd avoided until now.

If her body hadn't been perfect when she spent the night with Mark, it certainly wasn't now. Hollywood actresses might be able to reclaim their flat stomachs within weeks of having a baby, but she didn't have a trainer to whip her into shape and she'd been too tired to do a single crunch. Not to mention her belly had never been flat to begin with. Now it seemed unlikely to ever be.

She remembered when Mark had run his hand down her side, his fingers finding the bump there that she'd never been able to get rid of. She'd been so embarrassed, her face burning so much it almost hurt. And that had been with a stranger, someone whose opinion really shouldn't matter. The thought of Jake, whose opinion did mean something, seeing every ungainly lump and overly generous curve made her slightly queasy. Even now, as she reached for the hem of her shirt, the butterflies threatened to whip up a tornado in her stomach.

But as she pulled the shirt over her head and she felt the air wash over every floppy, stretched-out inch of belly, a strange calmness came over her and she didn't feel self-conscious. Precisely because this wasn't a stranger.

She let the shirt fall to the floor and stared up into his eyes.

There was no mystery there.

This was Jake. And he loved her.

That glow in his gaze warmed her. Reassured, she stood before him and simply let him look.

"You're beautiful," he said.

A different kind of embarrassment heated her cheeks. "You don't have to say that."

"I wouldn't say it if it wasn't true. And damned if I can think of anything else to say."

Far more than his words, it was the expression on his face that convinced her. No one had ever looked at her like that, with such gentleness, such caring, such desire.

Such love.

He held out his hand to her. Hungry for his warmth, his touch, she stepped toward him and placed her hand in his. As he moved forward to close the remaining distance between them, he wove his fingers through hers and clasped them together tightly. Something in her chest clutched hard and tears pricked the back of her eyes. Not of sadness, but joy.

When she'd found out that she was pregnant and decided to keep the baby, she'd thought about all the things, all the chances, she might be giving up, never knowing what she'd find.

To know love. To be loved.

To love.

Along with something she'd never dared hope for, sweeter than anything she'd ever imagined in fiction.

Her very own happy ending.

* * * * *

*Celebrate 60 years of pure reading
pleasure with Harlequin®!*

*Step back in time and enjoy a sneak
preview of an exciting anthology
from Harlequin® Historical with*
THE DIAMONDS OF WELBOURNE MANOR

This compelling anthology features three
stories about the outrageous Fitzmanning
sisters. Meet Annalise, who is never at a
loss for words… But that can change
with an unexpected encounter in the
forest.

*Available May 2009
from Harlequin® Historical.*

"I'm the illegitimate daughter of notoriously scandalous parents, Mr. Milford. Candidates for my hand are unlikely to be lining up at the gates."

"Don't be so quick to discount your charms, my dear. Or the charm of your substantial dowry. Or even your brothers' influence. There are as many reasons to marry as there are marriages."

Annalise snorted. "Oh, yes. Perhaps I shall marry for dynastic reasons, or perhaps for property or influence. After all, a loveless, practical marriage worked out so well for my mother."

"Well, you've routed me on that one. I can think of no suitable rejoinder." Ned rose to his feet and extended his hand. "And since that is the case, let me be the first to wish you a long and happy spinsterhood."

Her mouth gaped open. And then she laughed.

And he froze.

This was the first time, Ned realized. The first time he'd seen her eyes light up and her mouth curl. The first time he'd witnessed her features melded together in glorious accord to produce exquisite beauty.

Unbelievable what a change came over her face. Unheard of what effect her throaty, rasping laughter had on his body. It pounded a beat upon his ear, quickly taken up by his pulse. It echoed through him, finally residing in his stirring nether regions.

So easily she did it, awakened these sensations within him—without any apparent effort at all. And she had called him potentially dangerous? Clearly the intelligent thing for him to do would be to steer clear, to leave her to the tender ministrations of Lord Peter Blackthorne.

"You were right." She smiled up at him as she took his hand and climbed to her feet. "I do feel better."

Ah, well. When had he ever chosen the intelligent path?

He did not relinquish her hand. He used it

to pull her in, close enough that he could feel the warmth of her. "At the risk of repeating Lord Peter's mistake and anticipating too much—may I ask if you'll be my partner in battledore tomorrow?"

Her smiled dimmed. Her breath came a little faster. His own had gone shallow, as if he'd just run a race—and lost. He ran his gaze over the appealing lift of her brow and the curious angle of her chin. His index finger twitched.

"I should like that," she said.

His finger trembled again and he lifted it, traced the pink and tender shell of her ear, the unique sweep of her jaw. Her pulse leaped beneath her skin, triggering his own. Slowly he tilted her chin up, waiting for her to object, to step back, to slap his hand away.

She did none of those eminently sensible things. Which left him free to do the entirely impractical thing.

Baby soft, the skin of her lips. Her whole body trembled when he touched her there.

He leaned in. Her eyes closed, even as she stood straight against him, strung as tight as a bow. He pressed his mouth to hers. It was a soft kiss, sweet and chaste. And yet he was hot and hard and as ready as he'd ever been in his life.

She drew back a little. Sighed. Their breath mingled a moment before she slowly backed away.

"Oh," she breathed. Her dark eyes were full of wonder and something that looked like fear. He took a step toward her, but she only shook her head. His outstretched hand fell to his side as she turned to disappear into the wood. This was the first time, Ned realized. The first time, since he'd come to the house party at Welbourne Manor, that he'd seen her eyes light up.

* * * * *

Follow Ned and Annalise's story
in May 2009 in
THE DIAMONDS OF WELBOURNE MANOR
Available May 2009
from Harlequin® Historical

Available in the series romance section,
or in the historical romance section,
wherever books are sold.

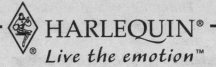

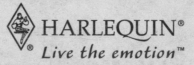

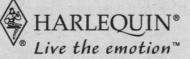

HARLEQUIN®

Super Romance®

...there's more to the story!

Superromance.
A *big* satisfying read about unforgettable
characters. Each month we offer *six* very different
stories that range from family drama to adventure
and mystery, from highly emotional stories to
romantic comedies—and much more! Stories
about people you'll believe in and care about.
Stories too compelling to put down....

Our authors are among today's *best* romance
writers. You'll find familiar names and talented
newcomers. Many of them are award winners—
and you'll see why!

If you want the biggest and best
in romance fiction, you'll get it
from Superromance!

Exciting, Emotional, Unexpected...

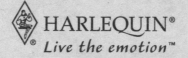

HARLEQUIN®
Live the emotion™

Harlequin® Historical
Historical Romantic Adventure!

Imagine a time of chivalrous knights and unconventional ladies, roguish rakes and impetuous heiresses, rugged cowboys and spirited frontierswomen— these rich and vivid tales will capture your imagination!

Harlequin Historical... they're too good to miss!

HHDIR06